# CHAPTER ONE

Rather than replace the battery in his watch when it dies, John Harvey decides to let go of time altogether. Either a few moments before coming to this conclusion or many years after, John is standing in his kitchen waiting for his coffee to warm while staring into the fist-sized hole in the wall next to the phone, one he had put there after his father, Major Harvey, called to tell him that his mother was gone. Heart failure. A result of her car accident.

It was the first time John had heard from Major in years, and it would be the last.

He informed John that Astrid's vehicle had been rear ended at a red light three days ago and pushed into the intersection of Union and Transit Road, where it was hit by a pickup truck going fifty-five miles per hour. John was as surprised by the news of her accident as he was by her death. He thinks that the jagged pieces of ripped drywall hanging behind the wall's surface look like teeth in the mouth of an eel. The driver of the truck was killed instantly. Astrid made it to the hospital where she held on for a little over thirty hours.

No, it looks more like a toothed vagina than a moray eel.

"Vagina Dentata," he says aloud, suddenly and without emotion, bringing to mind an entry from Wabash & Hudson's 1976 *Erotic Dictionary of Supernatural Mythology*. After Major Harvey broke the news to his only son in a low voice made tremulous by the many years it had gone unused, John went quiet and prepared for the ache to come. But the dense burst of numbness that had, at one point, managed to simultaneously fill and evacuate his mind only shrouded it now, the severity of its wrath lessened by his growing familiarity with despair, downgraded from boundless depths to merely innumerable ones. John once read that a tumor had the ability to turn into a different organ altogether, and in one case a doctor found an ear inside his patient's vagina. After some time, Major Harvey cleared his throat and began to speak. One more glassy-eyed plunge into an unwinnable war for the honor of a woman he had lost long before she left.

"She assst fer you," he slurred. "Wither las' breath my wife calls out forrer piece-a-shit son."

John thinks about the conditions necessary to grow a tooth. He wonders if it would be possible for one to emerge in, say, a nostril. Or a throat. John was not sure if his father had stopped talking or if he himself had lapsed into abstraction, but as he stood there in his kitchen holding the phone, the eye of his being saw his mother. She was upside down, death-bound, desperate and sorry, clamoring for the drifting earth with bony fingers while charmless fate dragged her toward the unseeable by her feet, her last word—his name—a refusal to concede to the universal necessity of decay and uttered as a plea with a pitiless closing door. Useless now, of course, though perhaps not always so. His mother wore the light blue coat that unfailingly appeared in

John's memories of her, a knee-length, velveteen peacoat he had again seen a few months ago when a toppled pile of papers in his bedroom revealed a picture of them together in front of her brother's cabin on their last trip there. It was the same coat he watched her put on five years before the trip while she stood at the front door saying to Major, in a voice that was simultaneously quiet and steadfast, that raising a child was more than she could handle by herself. His drinking was the cause of her yelling as much as it was an effect of it, but on that day everything was different. There was no screaming. There were no tears. There was only resignation. And as Major sat slouched on a kitchen chair, his red bathrobe barely covering his ogreish body, breathing heavy and wobbling with an empty brown bottle on the floor at his side and a lit cigarette propped up against the plastic black ash tray in front of him, Astrid very calmly told Major and herself and God that she was done. With what, John didn't know, but he watched from the stairs as she buttoned up the coat, repeating that one word over and over.

"Done."

Then the air left the room and a door was pulled shut behind it.

Astrid hadn't seen her son there, or if she did, she didn't acknowledge him. In the silence and the dimming light, a small John Harvey found that he was too confused to cry. There was something inside of him—something angrier than fear but further away—that he could not interpret without the key, the one that was now lost to him in the forest beyond the door. Without his guide, without any sense of direction, John pushed himself through the vacuum of space. Suddenly his room had appeared before him. He went in and closed the door behind him too.

John whiled away the time dreaming of her return. Eyes closed in his hard bed, envisioning vividly and distinctly every possible detail of her homecoming from the creak of the door when opening to the gentle closing of it behind her. From the almost inaudible friction of her fingers against the wooden buttons as she slipped them from their loops, to the whoosh of fabric as she let the coat fall from her hand against itself, toppling over the arm of the couch, and coming to rest, John saw all possible scenarios and meticulously recreated each one at the top of every hour like a model town, mentally adjusting only those few elements that depended on the time of her return. Things like the show on the TV, the position and location of his father's unconscious body, the amount of brown liquid left in the bottle, and the reach of the setting sun across the carpet.

As he was carefully piecing together the letters on the jacket of the fifth book from the left on the second shelf from the bottom to the right of the fireplace in the 7:00 p.m. version of the obvious world, John heard the sound of the door and the scene he constructed with a watchmaker's patience was set into motion. John followed the beat. Three steps to the hallway, sharp right turn, grab railing with right hand, touch every other step on the way down making six not twelve, father nowhere, bottle on the floor, local news, sports, sun butted up against the base of the wicker peacock chair on eastern wall, eyes wide, mother, beautiful, blue coat off.

She came to him and held him and wept and made a promise she would break more than once.

As John kneeled on his bedroom floor looking at that picture of himself standing in front of Astrid, both facing the camera, over-smiling, eyes squinted, her gentle arms draped across his shoulders, hands over his heart, so many years before the pain, before the monstrous words that gutted him of peace had been breathed foul into being, he thought that maybe it was her return that etched that blue coat into his memory and not her departure; the relief of seeing it come off brighter and more remarkable than the bewildering horror of watching it go on. With the tearful eye of his mind, he saw death finally overtake the defiant, struggling woman from the inside, a viral guide sneaking her over time to the intersection, slowly erasing her molecule-by-molecule as it burrowed through her body toward the core of the planet at a speed measured in days until finally she and what she wore and who she had been were gone, merging with air as a piece of glass might merge with the sea. But not what she said. That stays here. Swarms of black gnats putting holes in the light.

Hair, too. John read that doctors at the Cleveland Clinic had found a patch of hair on a tumor.

"A teratoma," he mutters aloud.

"Yer now the *bas*tard I always knew you were."

Major hung up the phone.

A tooth and an ear, both inside a vagina. Hair on a tumor. Such ugliness, John thinks, thriving secretly in your own internal darkness, stalking you, just waiting for one sinister thought to beckon it by name."

When the other end of the receiver went silent at 11:32 p.m. on Thursday, June 12, in the year 1985, John let the phone fall. He closed his eyes tightly to keep the pain at a distance immeasurable, and leaned against the wall with one hand, breathing loud and deep. He felt an untamed danger taking form beyond him, a dark puddle gnashing uncut teeth beneath language. His heart raced. Shrill, cold tones rattled at the base of his neck, muscles tensed against bulging corners of the tightening world. John grabbed the dangling phone in both hands. Helplessly shrinking and hyperaware. Dead-ended. Quicksand nasty cunt cruel useless sickfuck world. He screamed. In pain, at himself, for help, from Zola; voice cracking, vision blurring, louder, louder, pushing it toward his father at the other end of the quiet line. Beyond that even, across the once vacant canyon that stood between he and his mother that now, in her death, overflowed so abundantly with life that he could not see her. Fist clenched, John buried it in the wall. Punctured it. Suddenly there was air where formerly there was not. The abrupt calm of complete obliteration. His first taste was sweet.

No wonder life does it.

John never covered up the hole, leaving it and its teeth exposed. He did this partially to be reminded of the restorative properties of rage and partially to be reminded of his mother and father who still might be in there somewhere.

Maybe teeth could grow in a fist if it were closed tight enough. Long enough.

The surgeon squeezed an Ambu bag. Expanding and contracting. Filling and emptying. The deep red black on the blue gowns.

A few obligatory taps on the face of the instrument fail to reanimate it.

*Piece of shit asshole garbage come the fuck on I don't have time for this.*

The clock above the bed. Machines beeped frantically, unified in a wretched Greek chorus. Again, the clock. 2:10. Looking straight ahead, moving yet unmoved.

John unlatches the stainless-steel oyster link band.

*Fine. Fine. Okay. That's fine.*

Slides it down past his thick fingers.

*Okay. That's fine. Hahaha. Dumb fuck cheap trash. I'll just dump the food two minutes early today. They'll have to eat quick. It's fine. Totally fine.*

He felt the nurse's hand on his chest as she pushed him out of the room. The panic in Zola's eyes, a hand that reached longingly for him for the first time in months, maybe years.

John puts the limp watch on the checkered tiles of the kitchen floor.

That goddamned clock perched high above the chaos, quietly persisting, smug and oblivious to grief.

He reaches into a cupboard, grabs some Evan Williams, and pours it into the mug. One second, two seconds, three seconds. He thinks about the look on Steven Eastman's face as he slams the sharp coffee and puts the empty cup down next to all the others piled in the sink.

*Supply and fucking demand, the backbone of the most basic market economy.*

Steve extended the gift to John with a clumsily constructed glare of dutiful empathy. John looked down at him in disbelief.

"Fuck is this?" There was a rectangular box in Steve's hand.

"Please. Accept this as a thank you for your six years of dedication."

"Steve," John said, dismissing the severance gift completely, knowing that if he didn't take it the transaction was not complete. "Just think about this. Really think. Unlimited digital film? What value does that give to anyone's moments?" He still had a job for as long as Steve stood there holding the watch.

Steve shook his head. It was too late for this argument again. "I'm sorry, John."

John unplugs the white UltraVection Quickcooker next to his fridge and cradles it in his arms in a manner that could be described as loving.

"We have to let people go. This is nothing personal. Our department is hemorrhaging money." Steve wagged the box up and down and pushed it toward John's face.

John hoists the microwave up high above his head, pausing for a moment like a pendulum at the apex of its swing, towering over the timeless reminder.

He grabbed the watch from Steve and put a middle finger in his face.

"There's your Kodak moment, you fucking weasel."

John begins to bring the microwave down. At ninety degrees he is not dropping it toward the floor but pushing it with all of his strength, which is considerable. Zola is here. Eyes red and begging from across the room. Resentful. Astrid is seated across from John, her back to his new bride, smiling blankly, stone-faced, unaffected by the cries of the angry woman behind her. John is as he always was at times like this. Silent and useless, more a son than a husband, more an only child than a man.

"John, please!" Zola screams from the doorway. "Tell her. Show some fucking spine for once in your goddam life."

But John stays mute, shoulders hunched like a caught dog, and shamefully covers the cheap ring. He closes his eyes.

*And they shall say to the elders of his city, 'This our son is stubborn and…' Stubborn and what? Rude? Rebellious. Stubborn and rebellious. 'He will not obey our voice. He is a glutton and a drunkard. Then all the*

men of the city shall kill him with stones.' No, stone him to death. 'Stone
him to death with stones.' That seems weird. Stone him to death with
stones? Kind of redundant.

They are still closed when he hears the door slam.

His lamp will be put out in utter darkness.

When he opens them, only his mother remains. She is still
smiling. "Shall we get some lunch then?" she asks.

Who would want to remember everything?

The microwave crumbles against the ground. Both
mechanisms explode into unrelated pieces of shrapnel that
scatter in all directions, gears of different sizes liberated from
their orbits now spinning wildly away across the floor before
eventually coming to rest, farther from each other than they had
ever been before.

The last thing John Harvey is certain of is 6:54, 2/3/87.
He knows this because these are the numbers displayed in red on
the bedside alarm clock as John marches into his cluttered bedroom.
He steps over piles of yellow newspapers and lottery ticket stubs
and magazines and bills and letters and envelopes both opened and
unopened and books both read and unread, hulking and driven as
a Sherman tank. When he finally gets to the other side, he reaches
behind the nightstand and in one smooth motion yanks the cord
from the wall and hurls the digital clock directly into the center of
his own reflection in the dirty, frameless mirror above his dresser.
Glass spills everywhere. He didn't intend to break the mirror,
though if he were going to try to ignore time, he rationalizes,
perhaps he shouldn't be caught staring at its shadow.

Breathing heavy in the tense stillness that follows a sudden
crash, he looks down at the pieces of sharp reflective glass now

littering his crowded bedroom floor. Each one gives the illusion of a small opening carved into the clutter, portals poked out of the wasteland granting access to somewhere a little more organized, maybe. More symmetrical. John peers down into one of the new recesses, his long black hair surrounding his face like dark water falling away from a sea beast breaching the water's edge. He is reminded of his father with his hair the length it is. He thinks he should get a haircut. He knows he probably will not.

Heart beginning to slow, John's memory comes in through the front door of the rented apartment and moves through the smoky haze that hangs low over the living room, over the piles of yellow paged books and empty beer bottles and Styrofoam taqueria containers scattered on the ground around a worn dark green leather barrel chair brought up from the basement and put in the middle of the room, facing a console television set back against the wall. A spider plant wilts next to it in a white pot—not healthy, but salvageable. Behind the chair, under the dirty curtainless window, is an orange Bridgewater couch where John usually passes out in his clothes reading a book with one eye closed and the other fighting to stay true. A dirty pillow and a gray afghan that Zola had knitted while pregnant huddles along the left arm. The ordinary wooden coffee table in front of the couch now an ashtray and carved with shapes and letters that John apparently felt compelled to memorialize while in a stupor. He can't see what they say from here but he doubts they mean anything. Empty Michelob bottles stuffed with half-smoked cigarette butts that John stamped out after promising himself he would quit smoking. Walls white and dirty—bare, save the cobwebs.

No clocks. Clear.

He moves down the carpeted hall to the bedroom and peers in on himself standing on tiny slivers of broken glass among piles of newspapers and mail. On the walls around him are pictures cut from old magazines and handwritten phrases copied out of books onto Post-it notes, terms he wanted to look up or passages he found poetic—bible verses, new words, affirmations, equations, reminders that once he did more than just remember. He reads each one. A last look around. The window is dirty.

No clocks. Clear.

Back out into the hall and into a small bathroom. Half an inch of opaque water stands in the recessed white porcelain tub under an archway built into the wall to his left. A light blue shower curtain with some flowers on it that isn't long enough to keep shower water from running down it and soaking the floor, is pushed entirely aside. Above the toilet is a shelf with a fifth of peach Schnapps on it next to a stick of deodorant and three or four tubes of antifungal cream. There's a small garbage can between the clogged sink and the toilet that refuses to accept any more waste and a tube of Colgate toothpaste rolled up tight on the back of the toilet that has been empty for weeks but which John presses to the yellow, soft, errant bristles of his year-old toothbrush every morning anyway.

Clear.

He goes back out into the hall, past the door he barely opens anymore except to tidy the unused room behind it, and into the kitchen where he came from. Black-and-white linoleum floor covered in glass and white plastic. Sink full beneath a window overlooking a yard the size of a litter box next to the garage. Granite countertops running the perimeter of the room hidden by unopened mail and cards and newspapers and magazines and old lottery tickets piled up to the bottom of the class cabinets, in which there are four empty bottles. A space where the only clock had been. To the left of the entry: a phone. To the right of the phone: a hole. Across the room in the back right corner, a door to the basement that he doesn't go through.

Clear. Analysis complete.

Return to the present and John feels something strange.

Pride.

Something else, too.

Freedom.

John goes into the living room and sits on his couch and lights up a Marlboro cigarette. He smokes it slowly, almost sensually, reveling in a rare moment of self-satisfaction. Then he reaches over the side and grabs a newspaper from the floor. On the front page is an article about the space shuttle that has deployed a communications satellite to increase the amount of data transferred from space to ground. John reads it all. Then he grabs a pen and his stack of notecards and writes down "inertial upper stage booster" and "phase partitioning" and "tracking and data relay satellites" on three separate cards and tosses them onto the coffee table. He will look them up later. He puts the newspaper back on the floor and just sits there. For a while he thinks of nothing, but eventually decides he is dirty and wants to take a shower. Of course, he has been dirty for weeks, but being proud means knowing what to be ashamed about. Better view with a straight back. He stands up and goes to the bathroom.

John undresses and waits for the water to warm, his large body a home foreclosed upon by misfortune, abandoned and now giving way. Had he any reason to endure, he may have put some effort into its restoration instead of wasting his will on the tedious rehearsal of empty gestures while hovering somewhere between the pointlessness of life and the boredom of death. His days are long and vacant but for the most part they are at least painless now and certainly without fear, which in itself is a small blessing.

He sleeps restlessly until 6:20 a.m. every day and wakes in the same clothes he went to sleep in, having gone to sleep in the same clothes he spent the day in. At that time, he rises without alarm and begins a routine that is not loyal to any purpose, abiding a schedule that is not pursuant of any earthly need. Why, then? Because it does not matter. He performs these acts to prove to himself that habit does not conjure significance. He gets out of bed at 6:25 a.m. every morning, starts a pot of coffee, and plunges headlong into loss because patterns do not tease meaning from disorder. For this reason alone he opens the door that permits him access to a moment before grief. He does this only once a day. He vacuums the rug and cleans the mirror and straightens the cotton spines to remind himself that practice does not invent purpose in the same way that love is not summoned by a beating heart.

At 6:37 a.m., he closes the door behind him and puts the needle in the second groove of a record that never changes. When "Sound Chaser" starts, John goes into the kitchen, where he whisks an egg in a bowl of milk and adds a dash of nutmeg before pouring the bowl into a pan over a low flame. He then takes the toaster from the pantry and makes two small waffles. The eggs and the waffles will finish at exactly the same time—6:42 a.m.— giving Zola ten minutes to eat the eggs before leaving for work and the waffles enough time to cool to feed to his ornery child. While he waits for them to finish, he pours a fresh cup of coffee.

At 7:00 a.m., he dumps the uneaten food in the trash and the coffee in the sink and goes back to sleep.

John Harvey lives alone.

He does all of this to prove to himself that time adjusts in response to meaning, not in preparation for it. John's rituals are a spiteful mnemonic, a "fuck you" to everything that took away his joy. A gross revolt against hope, against the universe, against the idea that strength and bravery would have changed it all, against the thing he hated most: himself. John Harvey had been a grotesque mutation that spent atomic winter after eternal atomic winter barricaded in the fallout of cowardice and his routine reminds him that though he is finally fearless and undisguised, he is still just as helpless to an indifferent fate as ever. That suffering is his birthright.

In Zola, John had found life, golden and enduring, and for a brief and passionate hour he held her heart like a grail. Zola was to him the symbol and the word, the seeable meaning of creation itself, unfettered from care, unruled by judgments, as deeply knowing and determined as the roots of a tree. And she somehow, miraculously, saw her other half in him, in John Major Harvey, a hidden but imaginative man with no experience in the wild, no knowledge of anything other than knowledge itself, a keeper of facts and figures with no practice in the arts that Zola excelled in, things like being alive and being in love. But with her gone, the fire she lit was vanquished by a coarse wind that whipped around him both reckless and mad and in this crisp, palpable emptiness, the smooth curves she eased him into now revealed themselves as vulgar, menacing edges. In her love light he was touched and liberated. Out of it, he is now stranded. It shows on his face, too, in his half-shut eyes that gaze perpetually into the constant nothing.

John Harvey doesn't live anymore, he idles. He maintains his long crooked line of tiny, imperfect circles while waiting for the floor to drop out because he is too uninspired to kick the chair himself.

John ducks his head and steps over the side of the tub to stand under the weak stream of hot water. He is a tall man with bad posture and greasy, black shoulder-length hair. He weighs 282 pounds and his pinkish skin is shapeless and loose. He has a faded tattoo of a name on his left shoulder that he got on a whim and has regretted ever since. His beard is long and wiry and black with streaks of dark brown and red smattered throughout. His green eyes are small and the bags that hang from them are puffy and dark. Because of that, John usually wears sunglasses. They are black plastic aviators with a little gold mustang between the lenses that he got from the grocery store. Suffering from "Michelob Bloat," John's face is perpetually swollen and red, but between his sunglasses and all the hair, it is hard to see. John is fine with that. He smokes a lot of cigarettes and drinks heavily because of his father and all the arbitrary loss. He is disgusted by himself in every way, both inside and out. But as he begins to rub a cracked bar of soap across his flabby chest and into his armpits and over his distended, hairy stomach, John sees something he hasn't seen in months.

"Well, Dinah," he says, looking down at the glistening erection. "Today is your lucky day."

John was clever, obedient, and studious. When he graduated from the University of Buffalo's Engineering Department, thanks in no small part to an almost supernatural photographic memory, he was optimistic about his future. Not because he necessarily had any reason to be but because he hadn't really experienced a reason *not* to be. This callowness paid off. In the summer of 1980, less than a year after graduating, he was offered a job at a company in Rochester, New York, called Kodak, that specialized in producing imaging products. His parents (his mother, primarily) expressed her desire for him to work closer to home, but he ultimately decided that the position and the pay were worth sacrificing for. It was the first important decision he had made on his own and he was riddled with guilt the moment he recognized the want of his new, adult heart. To soften the blow for both himself and his mother, he promised Astrid that he would commute the forty-five minutes there and back every day instead of moving and she seemed not happy but accepting of the bargain.

On John's first day of work, he stepped out of the elevator and froze breathlessly in front of a secretary named Zola. She sat with her head in her hands as the doors opened. She wore a sleeveless, light green summer dress and had a round, Slavic face, high cheekbones, full pink lips, and a long, thin neck that she craned from side to side as she addressed, without a hint of enthusiasm, each man and woman scurrying past her toward their office. John thought her eyes were as blue and bright as the sky after a March snow, though she would later tell him that the hangover had just made them glassy. Her light brown hair twisted carelessly around a hairpin.

"You're lost," she said in a raspy voice as she closed her eyes and rubbed her temples.

"How can you tell?"

"Because you're still standing here."

John scratched his beard, something he did when nervous. "Yeah, I'm the new guy."

"Oh," she said. "John...something."

"John something."

"Ugh. Fine. Come with me, John something."

John leaves the shower and dries off with the same hardened towel hanging near the toilet that he always uses. His wet hair sticks to his shoulders underneath the neck of the XXXL plain black T-shirt he took off the floor that was ridged and wrinkled and marked with specks of old food. He knows that if he is to fuck Dinah, he will have to get drunk first. Not because she is necessarily unattractive but because he hasn't been with a woman since he and Zola conceived, and the last time he even saw a woman naked was during a botched threesome years later—a despicable memory that has left John repulsed by and ashamed of the idea of sex. But that morning, in the wake of the spontaneous explosion that violently defied the symbolic tyrannies of time, John feels in himself a new forward urging. A surge of primal electricity that fires him toward a magnetic point of heat somewhere in the deep unoccupied. He has a core, and this sudden lust reminds him that there was once a man around it.

When John and Zola learned in May of 1983 that they were pregnant, a seed that had been evolving inside John suddenly twitched, a barely legible pulse in the pit of his gut. She stood in the doorway of their bathroom with the test in hand and threw her arms around him. But there was something about her that felt false, something imperceptible but unmistakably present. It was when Zola let him go and stepped back that John caught it in her eyes.

Sadness.

No, something less human.

Uncertainty.

A stifling disquiet ravaged his mind. He was a hole upon which all of whirling space converged like an ocean's worth of sitting water on a sudden puncture. The unstoppable process of rot had begun, and John was very afraid. He had seen hell, and it was a blur.

Consumed by this new fear, John turned to what all those who are afraid inevitably turn to: faith. A shift from hoping to knowing, from an acceptance of every possibility to a denial of any. He disconnected from the truth. It was not her handwriting in that letter, he would tell himself, a misunderstanding. To protect himself against the dwindling that dashed beauty against the rocks, against the deterioration that set flame to our safest places, that forced his finished senses out the front door, there could be no letter. That's all there was to it. For the sake of his marriage, for the sake of their child, there could be no skepticism. Only faith. A total blindness. A darkness disguised as virtuous light.

He and Zola went for their final sonogram. To a man at risk, one anxious and artless, the signs of life on the screen might have been indistinguishable from those of certain death. But John was changed. He had a new commitment to the ever-expanding magnificence that sheltered only good and a duty to deny the importance of his own instinct. And so he kept his eyes fixated on perfection. He called upon faith to hold the gates closed behind him once he had stepped through. He brought Zola close and kissed her lovingly. He had never been happier.

John cannot imagine what the delivery room will look like or hear the doctor giving instructions as he urges a child into the world, but he has faith the birth will be ordinary. The doctor has to be the same short, round Indian man with gray hair that has overseen all of Zola's appointments, and there has to be an overnight bag that he packs himself in the reclining chair near the window.

And even though his view is obstructed by something so massive he cannot see around it, John has faith that he and his wife will look upon their new child and marvel at the splendor of his purity. Zola has to smile while he kisses her glistening forehead and his son has to wear a cap that his mother will knit as an act of mutually assured kindness.

And while John's mind cannot conjure up any shapes or forms or impressions, he has faith he will soon be spending his Saturdays at the same park by the lake that he visited in his youth. He and Zola will be sitting on the royal bench under a tree staring out at the water while his son plays in the grass. The bench has to be that same black curved-back steel bench, and the tree has to be the oak.

And though all of his humble focus and tight-lipped, hung-head genuflection refuses to reveal to him even the smallest detail of what that boy is or who he might become, John has faith that he will hear him call for John and see pure love in his eyes. His voice has to sound bright and warm like his mother's. The child's eyes have to be brown like his own.

But most importantly, despite the fact nothing comes into view no matter how high John looks, he has faith there is no reason to be afraid.

And yet John *was* afraid. He saw too much of too little not to be. Except, fear only exists in response to what approaches. So why then, when their son is strangled to death in the womb by his own umbilical cord, is John still scared? Darkness is upon him now. Once it falls, it cannot fall again. So what grief is yet to come?

But there is more pain in this world than John could comprehend. And he has lived so few lives.

Days later, Zola's body in the car.

The negative image of certainty isn't uncertainty. It is hopelessness.

John goes back to his bedroom and pulls on a thick, stiff pair of wool socks he pieces together off the floor and the crumbled Woolwich plaid flannel shirt he has worn every day for months. He walks through the kitchen, careful to not step on any broken glass, and once in the back hallway, he finds his insulated black leather Thermolite boots in the garbage for some reason, his faded black denim Levi jacket with a fake shearling collar on the floor, and his black winter hat stuffed in the mail slot. He is relieved to find the keys already in the jacket pocket since he cannot for the life of him remember coming home. John grabs the sunglasses he finds hanging from the plastic blinds on the back window, steps out onto the back porch, and locks the door behind him. It is snowing very hard. The sky is the same color as the air around him: a ceaseless gray hovering immovable over his exits. It is impossible for John to tell exactly where above him the sun is, but he squints into the sky as though he might be able to determine how much snow was up there, still left to fall. He either doesn't see anything or sees that it is infinite. Either way, John is not discouraged. He likes the snow.

Feels he belongs to it. In it.

John cannot bring himself to drive the car anymore, which he is especially thankful for today because without a clock radio he won't have to again face the minutes that are simultaneously building him into useless configurations and erasing him completely. He makes his way down the driveway, but when he reaches the end of it, he notices something across the street. She is barely visible, as usual, trudging along, her feet never leaving the ground, just shuffling on top of it, making long thin trails on the sidewalk that eventually alight behind her as the wind pushes them into new clouds. "The Woman in White," local legend, bundled from head to toe. Her white snow boots go up past her ankles, into which she's stuffed the ends of her white polyester snow pants. She wears her puffy white parka with white fur trim around the hood and over her mouth and nose a white scarf. A pair of white ski goggles covers her eyes. She carries in her white gloves three or four white plastic shopping bags full of what some people believe to be gauze and Kleenex and cotton swabs, but that has never been confirmed. As ever, the bags hang from her left hand, which is perpetually overlapped at her navel by her right as if she were solemnly paying her respects to something. Had she been able to stand upright, John guessed that she would have been about five feet tall, but not only was she always only in the distance, her spine was curved dramatically and set back a bit atop two very straight legs that never noticeably bent at the knees, giving her the appearance of a question mark or a sickle. No one has ever spoken to her nor has she made any attempt to speak to anyone else and she never faced any direction but straight ahead. She walks alone, always forward, and only in the winter. No apparent origin. No foreseeable destination.

As John stands with his fists balled up and thrust deep into his pockets, the Woman in White suddenly comes to a halt. John stops with her, cigarette dangling from his dry bottom lip, ears ringing in the horrible pitch of nervous machines. Without acknowledging his presence, and possibly even oblivious to it, she turns slowly and shambles off down the street from where she came until she is out of sight, fully submerged in an ocean of hard snow. John throws his cigarette onto the ground and stamps it out. Then he too enters the storm's depths.

# CHAPTER TWO

IN THE BITTER COLD OF A LAKE–EFFECT STORM, NATURE IS AT ITS most mute, the quiet of the entire city taking on its own dimension of width. John finds himself in such a storm that morning, all sheathed in teeth-white except for the blue-black hue of appalling silence. When the strange woman has completely disappeared from view, John begins walking in the general direction of Brinks, feeling the enormous pressure of the stillness on his face. He squints hard to discern anything in the distance, whether it be a traffic light or car or even another house, but he sees absolutely nothing. He debates going back inside and waiting it out, but as he has just used the last bit of whiskey in his coffee, his house is officially off-limits to him for the rest of the day. Plus, John knows that he doesn't need mile markers. He can turn off his mind completely and let the gravity of his beloved dark place pull him onward, lure him away from home, despite being snow-blind.

He arrives at the bar before any of the lights have been turned on. On the walk he sees no one and thinks of nothing he can even remember and despite the fact that his oasis of desperation was directly in front of him now, it was almost like he hadn't ventured there at all. John stands at the foot of the stairs leading to the front door, trying to mentally remake the morning's events according to the size of their duration, when three snowballs explode against the front window at the same time. John spins wildly to locate the kids that threw them. He sees nothing but the flurry.

"I know you, you filthy shit-rat motherfuckers!" he screams into the flat white wrath of a pale chasm. For a moment he debates giving chase, but when the blue neon "Brinks" sign flickers to life above the green door. John is reminded of his true purpose and abandons the hunt. Eyes squinted, he looks excitedly into the glow like the captain of a lost ship beholding land. To the right of the door in the large window is a simple neon replication of the Buffalo skyline and above that a vinyl flag advertising Genesee Cream Ale. Something about the door strikes John as strange.

In the memory of his first afternoon with Zola, he is holding open a black door. It is 4:00 p.m. on a Saturday. She is wearing a black hoodie over a pink shirt and light acid-washed jeans and white Converse high-top sneakers. Strands of hair have come loose from her barrette and fallen down around her neck. John puts his hand on the small of her back to guide her up the stairs but thinks he feels only cold, smooth stone. The door is black. Or green. The door is both black and green. On the other side of it will be a man and a woman, laughing. The man will grin hungrily at Zola and she will begin to disappear from at his side.

When John enters Brinks, he is surprised to find the guys already drinking.

"Jesus Christ, Orson. Did you not see me out there?"

"Out where?"

"Outside! On the goddam stairs," John yells. "Some kids were tryin' to friggin' pelt me with snowballs." He makes his way

past a man seated near the corner of the L-shaped bar with his
back to the door.

"You know I always sit right here, y'asshole. I ain't got eyes
inna back a' my head."

"Well how did you not see me when you were coming in
then?" John hollers now from across the room.

"Same way you didn't see *me* when *I* was coming in."

John stuffs his hat into his coat pocket, unbuttons the coat,
and sits at the place he has long ago marked with a knife, third
stool from the end.

"Hell of a storm, I guess."

"Hell of a storm," says Orson.

Brinks is old and meant for half-empty ugly people. There
is a pool table near the window that no one ever uses and a
grill behind the bar that no one ever cleans. The floor is sticky,
the walls are purple, and the lights are dim. They serve beer and
strong well drinks and nothing else. The song coming out of the
two speakers that hang from the ceiling behind the bar by the
cash register is "Valentine's Day" by a group called The Picnics.
John hates the song and it only makes his mood dourer. Dinah is
waiting for John in front of his usual seat.

"When did you guys repaint the door?"

"What? You think we do upkeep in this shithole? We have
never repainted anything," Dinah says. "We don't even plunge the
toilets. Whaddaya need?"

John pauses. "I'm looking for something full-bodied and rich
but not overwhelmed by an oaky mouthfeel. Today I think I'll try
a glass of the 1971 Condrieu AOC. What the fuck do you mean,
'what do I need'?"

Dinah rolls her eyes and throws a small white towel over her left shoulder. Then she goes back to the front of the bar, where the whiskey is. As she walks away, John looks at her ass, which he hasn't before. It is long and mostly flat except for at the very bottom of each side where it meets her leg and finally curves out just a bit like a heel in a sock. Nothing like Eleanor's, which had been firm and aligned.

John sat in a hard chair next to a striped couch in the living area of a large hotel room drinking a cold bottle of beer. In the years since Zola took everything with her, he had typically only left his house to restock his supply of alcohol and maybe grab some groceries and some cigarettes and a lottery ticket on the walk back while he at least had some savings left for his vices. He had no family anymore, never had any friends, and the couple whose Adam's Mark hotel suite he finds himself in currently were the last ones he remembers even noticing him. Eleanor visited often, even appeared in his dreams, but John was so perplexed by grief that he stopped answering the phone. Eventually she stopped calling. Spiraled outward along their divergent paths. Zola had been the one to pull them all together anyways. Without her, there was nothing to gravitate toward.

That particular Friday night marked the end of John's first week without job. He was at Brinks at 11:30 p.m., drinking harder than usual, watching the Sabres game that would end momentarily in an overtime draw with the Bruins. Dinah was trying to cheer him up by showing him a picture she took of herself in the mirror with her brand-new Polaroid camera.

"You do know I got fired from the company that makes these cheap pieces of shit, right?" he asks. "Do you think this is somehow helping me?"

"Just look at how pink it is still," she said, smacking his arm and putting the picture up to his face. "Like a trout's belly. Can't you at least put the tip in and wiggle it around for a few seconds? You literally have nothing else to lose."

"Still got my pride," he said.

"Trust me, you do not."

A bell rang and the door swung open. Eleanor and David, both in Sabres jerseys. John's heart pounded at the rare sight of her and he skipped a breath, the small part of him that looked back cautiously but fondly nagging now in his guts. It had been months, maybe even years, but she was exactly as he dreamt of her being. Laughing as she entered and looking back at David, Eleanor didn't immediately notice John. Though he longed to hear her voice again, he knew that there were too many things to atone for that he was in no shape or mood to atone for now. He tried hard to camouflage himself in the despair, letting his long hair fall in front of his face and pulling the collar up on his jacket and shifting his back to the door. He didn't want her to know him. This him. The one alive strictly to prove a point to no one but himself.

But he could feel her recognize him and when she did her laughter didn't just stop, it was sucked out of the room on backdraft. What exploded forward was the most awful sound in the world: his own name as said by a beautiful woman.

"John."

He slowly turned to face her. Her hair was different than he remembered it being. Shorter now, revealing the full breadth of her lips. He felt them on his cheek before she steps out of the car.

"I can't believe this. David, John is here. What are the odds?"

"Oh, wow. Hi, guys. Dammit," John stammered. "I was just on my way out."

Dinah put a bologna sandwich down in front of him and said, "Here's your bologna sandwich."

"What?" John laughed. "Dinah! I ordered this to go!"

Dinah looked at him like he was an asshole. "To go where? To the bathroom? You never leave this place." She turned to Eleanor. "What can I get you, honey?"

Eleanor ordered a gin and tonic. David ordered a rum and coke.

"Johnny boy. Good to see you." David put out his hand and shook it hard without looking John in the eye. Maybe he was disgusted by the sight of such lowliness. Maybe he pitied John, or maybe, like John, he knew that the only thing that they ever had in common was burnt up and locked away in a box somewhere in John's house and he saw no point in playing pretend.

David looked past John and saw a Greek man in a Hawaiian shirt playing darts. "Honey, gimme a few." He snagged his drink off the bar and excused himself.

Eleanor just stared.

"Hi, Eleanor." John took a swig of the last of his drink. It was warm and flat. "Been a minute."

"John," she said in disbelief. "It's so good to see you again. You look great. Finally put some weight back on. You look just like you did the day we met. That's a good thing."

John grunted and lit a cigarette. "Yeah, well. Don't let the good looks fool you. I'm dead inside."

"Stop it. How have you been?"

"Funny you should ask. Incredible, actually."

"Really? Oh, John, that's so good to hear. Tell me."

"Boy," John said, "where to begin? Well, as you know, my kid died and then my wife went into such a deep and irreconcilable depression that she killed herself in the garage of the apartment where I still live, yada yada yada. Old news, I know. But! Two years after *that* my estranged mother was in a car accident and when she died alone in the hospital a day later, my drunk father called to disown me."

Eleanor covered her lips with her hands. "Oh no. I'm so sorry."

"Oh, but wait. There's more! On Monday I lost my job!" He laughed manically and pounded the bar. "Can you believe it? Will the hits *ever* stop coming?"

"John..."

"But it's not all bad! Get this. See, I've determined that, considering I am definitely out of my parents' will, I still have enough money in my savings to last me seven months. Seven months to either drink myself to death or finally build up the nerve to blow my own brains out."

"John."

"You asked."

"I shouldn't have."

"Your turn now. I haven't seen you guys around at all. Not that I'm around much either, but, you know." He traced a tiny circle in the air with the bottom of his bottle. "Small town."

"Yeah, that's why we left it. Our careers didn't pan out like we thought they would. We moved back home."

"Uh-huh. Uh-huh," John said disingenuously, taking a long drag off of his cigarette. "But you and Dave are still pretending to love each other, I see. So that's good." He flagged down Dinah and motioned for another beer.

"We are. Yes. But judging by the looks of you, I'd say a fake love is better than a lost one."

She didn't know that John was no longer stirred by brutality. "Yeah, I bet," he replied calmly. "What isn't, though?"

Eleanor looked down and folded her arms, thinking she may have underestimated the stupid courage of the mortally wounded. John continued.

"So, have you intercepted any more letters between him and his soul mate? Or did those stop coming, maybe, I don't know, around the time my wife died?"

Silence. John turned his stool back around and faced the television.

"John, please. I have missed you so much. I wish I could have done more. There is not a day that goes by that I don't worry about you."

"Awww," John said. "How noble of you. But there is nothing to worry about. Really, I'm on a path. That's more than most people in this city can say for themselves."

David returned, sniffing. "All right, babe. Got an eight. Let's jet."

Eleanor didn't take her eyes off John. She knew if she left him now it may really be for good. "John, come with us," she demanded. "We have a room at the Adam's Mark for the weekend."

Though the sight of David produced a mental image of an anger that has suffered substantial generation loss, it was anger nonetheless, and John was still loyal to it.

"We have a fully stocked bar," she added.

John threw a ten on the bar and yelled toward Dinah, "Don't let anyone touch my bologna. I'll be back."

"I'll touch your bologna," Dinah said and went to high-five Ralph, who shook his head in disgust but put his hand up anyway because he hadn't made contact with a woman in over three decades.

At the hotel room, John ran through the checklist of perfunctory motions necessary to maintain a human interaction long enough to stave off a silence that would only echo Zola's name. It was the first time in years he had smelled Eleanor and let her voice burrow back through the abandoned coal mines of his heart. It felt nice. He hated to admit it, but it did.

Eleanor and David sat on the couch perpendicular to him that had a large blue-and-red-and-green checkerboard pattern on it. She had removed her oversized Perreault jersey to reveal a loose white T-shirt with "Niagara Falls" written in blue cursive across the entire front. She wore light blue jeans and curled her bare feet under her. She leaned over the right arm toward John, sipping a glass of Merlot while looking back over her left shoulder at David, who wore a white turtleneck. He was hunched over a mirror on the coffee table, snorting a thick line of cocaine he got from the only guy in Buffalo who deals it, a maniacal Greek nicknamed "Chef" who had the market cornered on thirty-five-dollar baggies of a laxative/drywall hybrid he cut up and sold to oblivious suburbanites looking for a downtown experience like the ones they saw in *Annie Hall*.

David finished the line and leaned his whole body back, tipping his head up to keep the heavy clumps of powder from tumbling out. "I'm tellin' you, we should write a movie about karate or magic or something," he said, pushing the mirror with five precut lines and a rolled-up ten toward John. No idea had ever sounded so terrible, but David's genuine stupidity helped tend to the wounds left in John by the thorns of envy and resentment. That he ever saw himself as inferior to such a fool made him feel just as foolish. No chance in hell Zola gave her heart to this idiot. There was nothing of her in him. John felt all of his muscles relax simultaneously, felt gravity loosen its grip on his feet. Zola was not here. Not in their voices, not in their mannerisms, not in the air around them. The storm had passed them over and as long as John stayed in their presence, he was safe from the winds her ghost rode.

"Oh, no thanks, man. I take my poison cold."

Dinah fills a glass with ice. On the television behind her is a soap opera, which means that it's a weekday. But which one? Days just smooth glass spheres stacked floor to ceiling with nothing inside or between.

"Honey?" David moved the mirror back toward her.

Eleanor looked at John for permission.

"No. No thanks. I'm good."

"More for me." David pulled the mirror back over to him. "Hey, John, I got a special effects guy I can call right now. We wouldn't even have to study. They can do all this shit with computers now. It's insane." He bent over to pull his next line and when his head was down Eleanor glared over at John, eyes wide. She reached out and rubbed the back of his hand that was wrapped around a beer.

David spread his sinuses open under his eyes across his cheekbones and sniffed. He said he'd run out of cigarettes and that he was going to walk to the store.

He stood by the door and told Eleanor to "give it a try."

John wondered what he meant.

Orson slides his empty beer bottle over to Dinah.

"Gimmie a second, Orson. You didn't even finish that one," Dinah says.

Eleanor smiled nervously. She was never nervous. Something was amiss.

*Holy shit. They're going to try to fuck me.*

John picked at the label on his bottle and tried to stop his hands from shaking.

"So," she said, standing up and positioning herself between John's legs.

"So," said John.

Eleanor looked down at him and smirked. Nothing about this was real, John told himself. It was a dream, one in which they had both evolved blindly over a landscape of separate griefs to finally meet. That their losses both perceived and real and their thoughtless lurches forward and their eras spent in between, petrified by doubt, would be timed so perfectly as to land them simultaneously in worlds hallucinated and true was just too fantastic to be taken seriously.

He set the empty beer bottle on the floor next to him and moved his nervous hands up to her waist. They decipher a welcomed unfamiliar. Eleanor bit her bottom lip and unbuttoned her jeans, snaring John with her eyes. She moved closer. Not like Zola would, he thought, surprised to find the name itself moved nothing when brought to mind. She bent down and clasped her hands together behind his neck. A new touch, one so inspired that John forgot everything and for the time being he was okay.

Eleanor stroked his hair. "My god, John. Where have you been?"

"Right in front of you," he said. "You just never noticed me."

"Well, I see you now." Eleanor kissed his forehead. "Better late than never."

John didn't agree. But it was not the time.

John put his hands under her shirt and rested them on the bare skin of her sides. Everything within him converged on that point of contact, that place where Zola blurred, and the things that once spoke of her finally began to speak of another. Their tongues were serious at play as she straddled him and worked herself into his lap. But he was too nervous to be aroused, too out of practice, and Eleanor could tell. She pulled back and stared at him forgivingly, then crossed her arms in front of her and brought her shirt up over her head.

"That's because it's warm down at the bottom," Orson says. He gives the bottle a shake.

"What about *him?*" John motioned with his head toward the door.

She leaned forward and kissed him again. John moved his hands over her bare back, her shoulders, her thighs, mapping her body. No matches on file.

*Fuck it.*

There had been nothing for so long. John let whatever it was take him to wherever it lived.

Bertie leans into Orson and says, "I bet she's warm at the bottom. That toasty little tush has been rode hard and put away burnt."

He put his hands on Eleanor's face, felt her hand on his. There was a different language now, more delicate, one that kept no record of Zola. Eleanor sighed. To John it spoke of love. Then the door. The inevitable, always opening door.

John threw his hands in the air and bolted to his feet. Eleanor fell back shirtless onto the ottoman but made no attempt to cover her body. David stood silent in the doorway. Just stood there, his mouth slightly open, eyes glazed over. The moonlight was the same color as his turtleneck. It pushed its way past him into the room and made it look like his head was floating in a sea of milk. He looked so dumb that John couldn't help but smile.

"You know what? You got me," he said, and laughed drunkenly half to himself. He reached down and grabbed a cigarette out of the pack on the table in front of the couch. "Red-handed." He lit it and looked over at Eleanor. "This was stupid. I shouldn't have come here." Back to Dave. "Well, bud, unless you want to kick my ass, I'm gonna get a cab back to Brinks."

"David, tell him it's okay," Eleanor said.

Her voice snapped David out of a trance. "Sorry, dude, I was thinking about some lyrics I wrote for our theme song. I'm really onto something. This is going to be great."

"David. Please, tell John this is okay."

David kicked off his shoes and walked through the living area toward the bed. "Relax, dude. It's cool. We do this shit all the time."

Dinah fills more than half the glass with whiskey. Splash of coke. Lemon wedge. Straw. Behind her, breaking news. Footage of the launch from Kennedy Space Center and the shuttle heading to orbit, followed up by the animated trajectory of the ship and some bullet points about something called CHAMP, which John can't read from where he sits.

No process or journey. John was just there. Appeared in the bedroom from nothing. When he came to, Eleanor was on her knees in front of him trying to make sense of the flaccid dick in her hand. John was shirtless, the belt and button and zipper on his dirty jeans undone. The moonlight sprawled across the bed. The red silk boxer shorts failed to hide David's erection. His short black hair was perfectly combed and his enormous chest heaved, covered in wiry black tufts.

"John, don't be nervous. Everything is okay. David. Please assure him."

David put out a cigarette into an ashtray at the bedside. "John, dude, I'm not even here. A fly on the wall. Go with it. Trust me, it's cool."

But it was not cool, and it wasn't David's presence that prevented him from giving Eleanor what she wanted. John knew there was meaning here, he could feel it moving somewhere underneath the heavy flesh. A heartbeat. He heard it. They deserved more.

Eleanor stood up and kissed John's neck.

"I can stay now," she whispered into his ear. She was asking him to remember her in that hotel room removed from clean and holy love. But in that memory she is warm. Down here she was dreadfully cold. Plastic.

"I can't. I'm sorry," he said. "Zola. It's just too…"

A burst of laugher from David interrupted John's phony excuse. "Zola?" he asked in disbelief.

Eleanor tried to signal to David that he should not say another word, but David was busy pulling another line.

"Dude, Zola had no problem with it." He inhaled hard. He rubbed his nose.

There began a grinding in John's chest, then a stammer, like a slipping transmission. "What do you mean?" he asked, though he already knew what it meant. Something was coming apart. Something had always been coming apart beneath him. He was just now noticing it at the surface.

"What I mean is that she definitely wun't thinkina you, so you might as well let her go."

Eleanor stepped back and narrowed her eyes. David shrugged and raised his enormous eyebrows across his sloped forehead.

"What?"

Certainties uncoiled and barreled toward a massive swirling vortex of throbbing wet muscle and fangs. At its bottom, death sprang to life. It chewed apart the fabric of John's past into pieces so small and angular they couldn't ever be reconstructed, his memories now as meaningless as his desires. From the bed of a valley in hell, John looked to Eleanor for direction.

"Zola was here? Where I am now?" Utter disbelief. Ears ringing. At thirty-five thousand feet, the tail of a plane is just gone. Screams sucked into the freezing blue. Cherished belongings thoughtlessly discarded into the vacuum of sky. Old truths processed through this revelation like wood through a chipper and spewed out behind him into particles of dust.

Zola smiles behind her desk. False.

Off the bus, unsparing beauty. False.

Laughter. False.

Touch. False.

Love. False.

Fate. False.

"No," David answered. "Different hotel."

John had taken himself hostage. Eleanor moved toward him very carefully. "John, listen to me. Look at me. It was harmless fun. It meant nothing. I promise you. We just played around."

He rubbed his eyes and stepped back. "I can't fucking believe this," he said, his voice shaking. "Why would you tempt her? Why would you let me go on loving her and not tell me what she was capable of? I thought you guys were my friends."

"Dude," David interjected. "You started making out with Ellie the minute I left. Don't act like you're better than us."

John stayed silent. He wanted to but couldn't say why it was not what it had looked like. That it had meaning.

"I know what this is," he said. "This is revenge. Petty fucking revenge."

"Revenge?" David laughed. "Revenge for what? You think Eleanor is trying to get back at me for hooking up with someone else? The girls were going at it too, chief. Should'a seen 'em. Ain't that right, baby?"

Eleanor shook her head shamefully; let it hang.

Jaw clenched, muscles trembling, John glared over at David, who bent over to inhale another line. Eleanor put her hand on John's face to bring him back to her, but he threw her off.

No, not revenge for lust. Revenge for love. Eleanor wanted to know what the two feel like together. She wanted to feel what David felt with whoever it was that he felt it with. And she wanted to do it with David watching.

"John, no," Eleanor said. "It's not. In here and out there are two very different things. This is just something we do… underneath. Apart from real life." She spoke slow and succinct, the language one uses when forced to talk loudly about a secret, drawing a map with her tone, leaving clues in the pauses. "It doesn't count against us here."

John immediately tossed aside any nuance she may have been trying to attach to the word "us."

"Oh?" he asked incredulously. "Because it seemed to count when you found that letter. Remember when you realized love seeped out of your little 'sexual aside' here and poisoned your real life? It sure as fuck looked like it counted then."

"What letter? What are you guys even talking about?" David asked. "If we can't get this moving, I'm going to go jerk off in the bathroom."

"David!" Eleanor yelled. "Please."

"Fine. I'll do it here. I don't care." David lay back and reached into his boxer shorts and began toying with his cock.

"When," John said, not so much to Eleanor but through her.

"John."

"When did this happen, Eleanor? I want to know the exact moment I lost her."

"John, please."

"WHEN!"

Eleanor sighed. "You never really had her."

"Fuck you."

David jumped to his feet.

"Dave," John responded calmly, "so help me god, you take another step and I'm going to stab you to death with one of your own broken teeth."

David called his bluff and John, having never thrown a punch in his life, stunned him with a left-handed slap before hitting him shockingly hard with a right across the jaw. Eleanor was screaming now and David, sobered by the attack, grabbed John by the shoulders and flipped him clear over the top of him with his right leg. John was amazed by the strength it must have taken to get a man of his size airborne and crashed hard between the wall and the bed under the window. He could not get to his feet before David had every advantage a coked-up sex maniac could hope for. In the moonlight, John pictures David's erect penis as an illuminated spear in the hand and in the mouth of the woman he loved.

Loves.

He screamed. The shriek of a scared animal, coming from somewhere further away than that moment and carrying with it so much more than just pain.

David seemed briefly bewildered but got his bearings and hit John once with his blunt fist, his enormous, pendulous dick swinging in time beneath his loose boxers with each inhumanly solid blow, his confused rage fueled by the drugs he had inhaled. John had always thought coke was supposed to make your dick smaller and wondered how much more deceit he would be forced to confront that night.

Dinah says, "Shut the fuck up, Bertie," as she stands at the register starting John's written tab. Bertie laughs. Bertie is an African American man in his fifties. He walks with a limp and has a peace sign dangling from his left ear and wears the same old brown leather jacket and gray wool newsie hat every day no matter the weather.

Though one eye had already begun to swell shut, John could see David looming over him now, glowing in the light of the moon that hovered at the top of the sky outside the window, observing the indecency but doing nothing to stop it.

"Don't make me hit you anymore, John," David yelled, but John had lost everything and there was no sense in him ending his last chance at fury one second before he absolutely had to. He spit blood into David's face and it sent him reeling backward.

"Goddammit, dude! Stop already!"

Falsely believing himself to have just gained the upper hand, he tried to get himself to his feet but they were still above him and his head was partially under the frame of the mattress and his soft penis had fallen out and his saggy pale flesh was everywhere. In his shame and disgust, John chose instead just to die. Right then and there, bloody and half naked. He saw no use in fighting anymore. No point in standing up. What was left there for him at eye level anyway? Sinkholes. Complex memories revealed as simple, childish optical illusions. Cruel tricks of the light played on the sleepless by a pale moon and its waves, lens flares, particles of dust, fleeting and inconsequential.

John groaned and pushed his tongue against his canine. It was loose.

"Stay down, John! Please. I don't want to hurt you," David yelled again, wiping blood out of his eye with his bicep.

Angry, confused, and utterly humiliated, John slowly stood up in the thick fog of ash. Eleanor watched him sadly, shaking her head in disbelief while David paced the room like an animal that had been caged and gone insane. "I think it's best if you leave," he said.

"Oh, do you really?" John asked as he gathered his clothing. "So I can't still get a quickie?" He swiped his last possession off the floor and moved to the door of the hotel room. His heart was gone and with it all propriety—one perk of no longer fearing an outcome.

"By the way," John said to Eleanor, "it was Zola's handwriting."

She glared at him curiously.

"The letter to Dave? It was from Zola. They apparently stepped out of the sexual shadow you thought you all could hide in."

John took a moment to absorb the image before him, the last one he would ever have of Eleanor, a scene of pure potential, the nanosecond before a fired object tears apart its target. The final breath of peace. Then he closed the door behind him. He carried nothing. He had no one left to lose. He was a castaway, seen only from a distance by the black-eyed creatures that inhabited his island—untouchable, fearful little bastards that paid him no mind until he moved closer.

But he no longer dared to move closer.

Dinah sets down the drink. John wraps both his hands around it like a weapon and looks down in, lost among the forests of the world.

"Big man," Bertie yells to the end of the bar.

John looks up, confused.

"Where the hell you been?"

The space around John begins to take the form of a barroom. He moves his tooth back and forth with his tongue. Still loose. Just slightly.

"Whaddaya mean?" John asks. "I'm always ahead of schedule." He has emerged unscathed, but to be completely sure, he empties the glass down his throat in four enormous gulps, dries his lips, and motions for Dinah to get him another.

"Puttin' 'em back awful quick today, John!" she says. "Devil must be right on your heels."

"Not today you're not," says Bertie.

John winces as he tries to make sure the drink stays down. "Well, then." John suppresses a vomit-filled burp. "I guess you'll just have to forgive me, old man. I ain't keepin' tracka time no more."

Bertie stands up and hobbles over to John. He sits down next to him. "You did what now? You stopped keeping track of time?"

"I did."

"Why would you go and do something like that?"

John lights up a cigarette. "Because fuck it. It takes without permission and it doesn't give nothing back."

"Do you think it's wise to toy with the universe, John? Given your—" Bertie pauses to choose the words carefully "—past dealings with it?"

"Don't start with that." John exhales. "Time is the toy. Who gives a shit what I do with it?"

Dinah sets down another drink.

"Oh no, no, no, you got that all fucked up, John Harvey. Time is how life takes attendance. And if you're absent?" Bertie shakes his head and stands up. "I pity the fool."

"What the hell does 'I pity the fool' mean?"

"Saw it in a movie. Means I feel bad for you because you're stupid."

"What movie?"

"*Rocky 3*," he says proudly, like he made the movie himself or unearthed it from an ancient tomb.

"They made another one about the boxer?"

"Yessir."

"Why do you watch that shit?" John asks.

Bertie looks confused. "Because a man has got to fight."

John shakes his head. "No. No, he don't gotta fight at all. A man *could* just stay down. He *could* just die. I mean, you're gonna die anyways. Why not save yourself the trouble?"

"Well, I suppose. But a boxer's got ten seconds to figure out what kinda man he is."

"There you go. Exactly my point. He's got ten seconds to assess his values? And under such duress? That ain't even enough time to decide what kinda pop you want from the fridge when you got *no* one countin' on you. How can you ever be sure you made the right decision? Go down early, stay down for good. That's my take. It's a race to the end. Get yourself a head start."

"Well? You ain't Rocky."

"Goddamn right. Good."

Bertie waves him off.

"Look," John goes on. "All I'm sayin' is that without time, I bet I have all the time in the world."

"Oh? Tell me something then," Bertie responds. "What time do you think it is right now?" He pounds his thick finger down on the bar top.

"Okay, well, I was awake at six twenty as always," John begins. "I remember the clock in my bedroom said six fifty-four a.m. after I destroyed my microwave, which I will definitely need to replace if I ever want to eat pizza rolls again. Then what? Took a shower." John winks at Dinah who winks back. "Got dressed. Went outside. Oh, I seen that weird woman! Couldn't a' watched her for more than a few minutes. Got to the bar where I was almost hit with them fuckin' snowballs no thanks to you guys, then the lights came on." John does some calculations in his head. "So it's gotta be about ten thirty a.m."

"Ten thirty. You say it's ten thirty."

"Yeah. Let's say ten thirty-five."

"Oh, you poor, dumb, hooky-playin' son of a bitch," Bertie cackles with delight.

"What? What the fuck is so funny?"

Bertie stands up and hobbles back to his own seat. "It's already forgetting you."

"Well, what time is it then?" John yells after him. Bertie just laughs again and sits down, turning his stool to Orson. "You asshole," John says. "Dinah. Dinah. Come here. What time is it?"

"No idea, hun. I don't wear a watch when I'm working. Makes the shift drag. All I care about is seeing my replacement walk through that door."

"Don't you have a clock in here?"

"Yeah," she says. "Like we want to remind these people that they should probably be somewhere else."

# CHAPTER THREE

WHEN THE WORLD BEGINS HUMMING AS ONLY A THIRD DRINK will cause it to, Dinah emerges from behind her plume of fearless lust as rare stone and the things that usually kind of repulse John about her he now sees as thorns around some precious fruit. Dinah had made it clear she wanted John to fuck her, and it wasn't just in the way she looked at him and smiled or poured his drinks with an extra heavy hand or laughed obnoxiously at his rusty attempts at humor. It was the way she loudly and repeatedly told him that she wanted him to fuck her. Overtly horny, she embarrasses John Harvey, who has a reputation for being a serious man among the local drunks. They know of his troubles and care for him in a way that only displaced strangers can. Bertie and Orson and Leo and Ralph are protective of John and make him feel safe in their island kingdom of emotional squalor. They are clumsy and brash and carry inside of them a feral storm, but every day they huddle together in dizzy mourning above and around their fragile friend while the tempests they cannot tame with drink pass outside. It is the most stability John can hope for anymore. He is thankful for them, mostly, but he does sometimes feel pinned him down by their pity, the sympathetic eyes of those he knew and those who only knew of him weighing so heavily on his back that even if he had wanted to stand upright, he could not. Also, that a loose assemblage of miscreants, divorcés, and most likely perverts feel bad for *him* is not something that does John's long-depleted sense of self-worth any favors.

She had removed her oversized light blue BUM Equipment crew neck sweatshirt to reveal a ribbed white tank top, the front of which she had tied into a knot above her navel. Her breasts were large and her bra kept them nestled tightly at her bottom ribs. Her belly hung a little over the waistline of her dark, stonewashed jeans but her arms were firm from her years of hauling beer from the basement cooler to the bar. Her hair was long and brown and wavy and pulled back into a loose ponytail held in place by a dirty white scrunchie, which made it easier to see her thick, well-sculpted eyebrows and the lines in her face. John has no idea how old she is. She could be in her fifties as easily as her thirties.

The bar is crowded for a weekday afternoon, and Dinah has not been able to flirt with John as much as she usually does. Normally this would have been a relief. Today it makes him want her more. He watches hungrily as she strains to open a bottle for a pale, lanky, balding man wearing a long black trench coat. When she sees John staring, she smiles and walks over to him, the confidence in her strut almost sexy.

"My pussy is just as tight as my asshole," she says as she leans on both elbows in front of him, giving him a clear view down the front of her shirt.

"Jesus Christ, Dinah."

"Don't go using that name too much just yet. He'll think you're crying wolf when you're yelling it later. You want another drink or something? I seen you eyein' me up."

"I do," John answers, "but I think I need to get some smokes and something to eat first."

"I got something you can eat."

John tries to hide his amusement.

"Don't judge me, John Harvey!" Dinah exclaims, playfully slapping the back of his hand. She straightens her shoulders and begins to recite: "'We cannot be judged by what we do, only what we keep ourselves from doing.'" Her voice is smoky and harsh enough to drive a nail into leather. "Andrew Clark said that."

"The fuck is Andrew Clark?"

"The famous writer? Andrew Clark! I can't believe you've never heard of him! An' I thought you was a bookworm."

"His name is Clark Andrews," he says. "And you got the quote wrong. What he actually said was, 'We will only be judged by what we do. Not what we refrain from doing.'"

"Same thing."

"Not at all the same thing. You changed it to suit you better."

"So?"

"I'm going to the store for some cigarettes. Start me up a sandwich, huh?"

"Hold on. Gentleman at the end of the bar down there wanted to buy you a shot." She pulls a dirty shot glass from beneath her and pours too much whiskey into it, spilling it down the sides. John looks but sees no one.

"Who? Orson?"

"No, other guy." Dinah motions toward the front of the room but when she looks she too sees nobody there. "He's probably taking a piss." John raises the glass to the empty space the man had once occupied in a ceremonial gesture and downs it.

"Keep my food warm 'til I get back."

"Your meat will be hot. You have my word."

"You're a piece of work"

"I'm a goddamn masterpiece."

There is a couple playing pool. John has never seen anyone use the pool table before so he is intrigued enough to stop and observe. He leans against the side wall and lights up another cigarette. The man is older than John and has greasy, curled black hair and a thick mustache. He is wearing a denim jacket with an upturned collar over a mustard-yellow T-shirt. His much younger girlfriend sits on a bench that runs along the wall at the foot of the table. Her skin is dark and her hair is shiny and long. She anxiously taps her foot and eyes her boyfriend. She is wearing a white flare dress and black satin pumps and doesn't look like the kind of person that would normally frequent Brinks. John thinks she's more of a "four-star-hotel lobby bar" drinker.

The man says, "You're about to see an expert at work," and smirks like a creep. He has a gold cap on his incisor tooth. The guy then puts the balls in a wooden rack and rolls it back and forth a few times before positioning it at the head. He pulls the triangle off and tosses it onto a card table in the corner, where his cigarette burns in a tray. Then he walks to the foot spot and puts the cue ball down.

"I mean I honestly wouldn't know the difference," John replies, unfazed.

"Show 'em, baby!" yells the woman, an exclamation that takes her boyfriend by surprise. He turns around and bends over and kisses her passionately.

John winces.

They eventually stop kissing and the man returns to the table to line up his shot. When he strikes the cue ball, it explodes off the tip like it was fired out of a gun and it hits the one-ball at the top of the pyramid directly in the center. With a deafening bang, the strange English applied causes the ball to career off the one at a perfect right angle into the rail closest to John directly at the diamond before bouncing back toward the center in another straight line.

The doctor came out into the hall. John thought he looked too calm, a man who had the only answer needed. When the word "suffocated" seized the moment, it spread like cancer, infecting every second in a million-year radius. The balls scatter across the table. The eleven, thirteen, and fourteen balls hit the back rail at different spots and burst toward the front where the greasy man is standing, staring at John with wide eyes. The cue ball continues in a straight line, untouched by the random trajectories surrounding it like a ship traversing a meteor shower. Sun snuffed out, sky empty. John saw the doctor put his hand on his shoulder but didn't feel it. The cue ball comes back toward John with the same force it had left him and along the same straight line. The twelve crosses the cue ball's path behind it as the six hits the top corner of the side pocket and speeds down past it just up ahead. John is conscious at the pinnacle of a deep grief.

His instinct was to flee the blast radius, to run in any direction from the ground zero that was unwittingly made of his center and not stop until he was a hundred years way but his legs were weak and John knew he was trapped firmly in the moment forever. He could not plead his way out of the unbearable process of loss for life is a deaf tyrant and it is unmoved by tears. If he could, he would have simply erased himself from history. He would have given it all back to unsee the pain, pluck his body up out of the series of small glories that brought him to that conclusion under the pretense of witnessing just one miracle, and wipe all memories of the wretched John Harvey from the record the hospital clock had been keeping. Shouldn't that be his bargain to make? Aren't men owed that much?

John knew then that he had been duped by faith, lured out into the world by the promise of peace and curative love. This is where trust brought him? A foreign land in the freezing cold, left to face anguish with no weapon? He should have known better. He should have known faith was nothing more than the battle cry of those without a strategy. It will not save. It does not prepare. It is a false positive.

The fifteen collides head-on with the seven and both veer back from where they came, having absorbed each other's force. The woman smiles and nods as she watches from her seated position. Who really does death happen to? Those it takes or those it takes from? The four ball bounces off the bottom rail and smashes into the back of the ten, putting it directly into the path of the five. John is reminded of being in the back seat of his mother's purple Ford Grenada in the summer of 1961 on a trip to their uncle's simple three-room log cabin with a purlin roof built by his uncle's hand on ten acres in Varysburg, New York, a place completely isolated from the world around it.

No, it was not the Grenada, he thinks. It couldn't have been. The Grenada would arrive much later and last only until it reached an intersection under a red light. John is confused why he can only see that car parked along a gravel path when the trees end, though he knows it was not the one that was there. On the ride up, John and his mother are singing along to a song on the radio. Something by The Picnics. He can hear the melody but he cannot remember the words. She is laughing. John's father is missing from the memory. He is missing from most memories, and if he is there he exists in the periphery, like a faint star that only blinks when your eyes are drawn to the brighter star next to it.

Except for one. There is one memory in which Major appears boldly.

John was ten. His mother was out for the day, so he was left in his father's care, which meant John was alone in his room quietly reading a book.

Suddenly the door opened. His father.

John was startled at the sight of him upright and fully clothed. Major told him to get in the car, said they were "goin' boobin'," and winked. John hadn't the slightest idea what this meant but was exhilarated all the same at the notion of spending time with his dad and honored to have been chosen as a partner on such an important task. He ran down the stairs, out of the house, and hurriedly buckled himself into the front seat of the family Ford.

As they backed out of the driveway, Major said that first they would have to make a quick stop. Ten quiet minutes later, they pulled into the parking lot of a liquor store. Major cracked a window, turned the car off, and went inside, leaving John to imagine what the rest of the day might consist of. Something elite, he assumed, particularly if his mother was not invited. A game, maybe. A hunt.

Major returned with a bottle of whiskey. Holding it proudly in front of him and allowing the sunlight to seep through it, he turned to John and said, "Daddy's gotta have his boobin' juice," then put the car in drive.

John was happier than he ever remembered being.

When they arrived at Delaware Park, Major put the bottle in a brown paper bag and escorted John by the hand to a bench along the walking path that circled an enormous pond. The hand was hard and the grip was firm. It made John feel invincible, like an extension of a spectacular machine.

"Have a seat, little man," Major said. Every word out of his mouth that wasn't crooked or seething with anger caressed John's small heart. He was cotton-soft and full of light. John sat down next to his dad and looked up at him, squinting hard at the man seated between him and the sun, awaiting instructions. Major pulled a pair of cheap sunglasses out of his shirt pocket and put them on. He pushed his long hair away from his face with both dirty hands and glared intently down the bike path. Then he froze. He did not move a muscle, did not make a sound. John stared, too, though he wasn't sure what he was looking for. After three minutes a woman appeared—a jogger—seemingly borne of thin air by Major's concentration alone. He took a sip of whiskey and repositioned himself. Spine straight. Eyes directly ahead.

John did the same.

When the woman ran past them, Major nudged John with his elbow. "Lookit them boobs."

John exploded into embarrassed laughter and covered his face with his hands. Major took another swig. John recognized the sweet, piercing stench of alcohol. Major put his hand on the crown of John's head and moved his entire small body back and forth. Then he laughed from deep within his round belly. It was a sound John had never heard before. It was beautiful and warm, and he knew that if he could only crawl inside of it, he would be safe forever.

On the first night at the cabin, the adults get drunk on whiskey while the two boys play inside. They work up a sweat and John opens the window.

On the second night, an ash from the bonfire is carried by the wind through the front window that John forgot to close. The ash lands on the curtain behind the five of them as they all sit upwind from the campfire smoke facing the moon. It ignites the curtain and the chair in front of it before moving across the old rug to the kitchen table, which it hops on to touch the ceiling. No one knows it was there until the crackling sound of a flame snapping the bones of the roof gets his mother's attention. By then it is too late. The remoteness of the cabin, the very reason they cherished it, was what guaranteed it would not survive. John can do nothing but stand in the yard and look at the fire feasting on the shelter, waiting for what seems like an entire lifetime. Eventually it grows full. When the water arrives, there is nothing that can be salvaged.

In the days that followed, Zola would lean toward sickness while John bent toward despair. The one and eight are both rolling toward the left side at angles and they barely touch, but when they do they split from each other in a V shape. John sat next to her bed for hours at a time, the silence of despondency so much more important than the months of shrieking unease. He contemplated her as she glared out the window of the fourth-floor hospital room, listless but focused on the hard February sky, wrestling with an indecipherable carving on its inside walls for hours at a time, stopping only to sleep. He thought her to be more real in her suffering than she had been in the entirety of her zealous bliss. Here she was vulnerable to true love, not just idolatry. Seeing her in this condition made John ashamed of giving his uncertainties an audience for so long. He promised himself in something like prayer that if she would only come home, he could see just the beauty. That he now knew exactly where to look.

But Zola's sleep was violent and John knew that not even her dreams could keep her safe from the driving winds anymore. They could not shield her from the pummeling rain that slated the thirst of the days that only devoured. Her waking moments were not extensions of the fantastic as they had been in the early days and weeks of their affair. Her sleep no longer a harbor. There was a hole in the bow of her slumber where the anguish of the world flooded in and had anyone actually seen her it would have been obvious that Zola was damned. But no one could. The cue ball hits the same point on the rail in front of John as it did off the break and again moves back to the other side through the center, untouched.

For John, time would eventually begin again. There would be two or three seconds in every hour instead of just one. But for Zola the opposite was true. Her days were twenty years long, every second housing hours and hours of insufferable agony and by the time she was released to go home four days after losing her child, she was old and tired and ready for death.

John takes another drag of his cigarette. The man looks over at him and nods, pleased to discover his impressive break is still being admired. More than just admiring it, John is spellbound.

After returning home from the small service held for their son at the church in the hospital, John woke up to use the bathroom and heard a car running. The sound was close but muffled. Zola was not in bed with him.

He already knew. He could already see it.

Though it was too late, John ran down the hallway to the door in the kitchen that went out to the backyard and threw open the garage. An abyss. The ribs around the heart of dread. Murky gray fumes swirled in a desperate search for form. He began to wade toward the vehicle through the thick, pungent clouds of tar, the moon behind him a useless headlight in a dust storm. As he fumbled around in the suffocating chasm, he could vaguely make out only more roiling hues of black.

Lake Erie invited John closer. He looked back and saw his mother, smiling into the sun, impervious to the death ahead of him at the place where the water met the land, the death that waited to greet him, to take him in, to change him, and spit him back as something different. There is an animal trapped between the rocks. It was beautiful once, but by the time he finds it, it will have decayed. If it is to be seen, it has to be.

The doors were locked.

"Be careful," said Astrid.

John pulled off his T-shirt. He wrapped it around his fist and put it through the driver's side window. Then he popped the lock, uncoiled the shirt, and put it over his mouth and nose.

The bones were there for him to find and they would call for him until he did.

John leaned into the car and turned off the engine. With the clear night air diluting the haze, a picture emerged. Her face, eyes closed in the passenger seat. Two empty bottles of prescription pills on the dashboard in front of her. Just in case. In the corner of her mouth, a thin white foam.

Doom.

That's the word.

After the ceremony at City Hall, John and Zola snuck away to a Casino Hotel in Niagara Falls, where it rained for three days straight, the thick clouds outside their honeymoon suite window crept seamlessly into the mist around the mouth of the river. The froth there gathered on the rocks at the bottom of the gorge and equalized the impressive distances into a glazed marble wall. Too full of young love to let the weather sadden them, they spent most of their time fucking and gambling and drinking in the lobby bar with other guests. Newlyweds mostly, broke and secretive, too. A man and a woman from Ithaca, a little older than John and Zola but equally matched in vitality. He played the guitar and she waited tables.

The sun went down while John stood at the bar watching his new bride from across the room. He was amazed at the mastery her animal soul had over every human cell it had been given. He admired the way she moved it through the world instinctually, on a breeze—liberated from concern, trusting of the odd, sometimes cruel patterns of a stubborn fate, in harmony with the glitches and nervous ticks of an anxious universe. Her vehicle, the name and notion of Zola Lumi, was the shape of the track it traveled, the exact dimensions of the path forged by time. It could go no other way but smoothly onward, carried by momentum not toward a mortal end but toward a horizon that always receded, calling to her playfully but staying out of reach. Her spirit had evolved into the being that life found most beautiful, its colors the brightest, its song the loudest, its dance the most exotic, and so life evolved toward it as those in love and driven only by a need to create are built to do. As John himself now did. He considered himself the luckiest man in the world.

But on their second night there, John saw Zola turn a corner toward the bathrooms with the twenty-five-year-old musician who had just married the waitress. He wore white linen pants and a red short-sleeve button-down. He had carefully careless jet-black hair and a tattoo on his forearm of a snake. As he and Zola were about to vanish from sight, John thought he saw her take his hand. He looked across the bar. The waitress was wiping a tear away from her eye with the bottom of her palm.

The negative image of hope isn't hopelessness. It is uncertainty.

John was sitting in the driver's seat next to his wife, a chosen witness to the vivid unseen.

The cue ball again begins its return toward John with the same speed it has maintained since the break.

John moved his fear of all like an arrow of glass through his hard, still heart. And when it was beyond, there was nothing left but a hopelessness sculpted by a master's hand and the conviction that all struggle is mute and goes unseen.

John let their bodies stay there in the quiet for some time. When the noxious fumes of exhaust dissipated, he went inside to call an ambulance. The paramedics arrived and John said she was gone when he found her. He did not tell them about her thumb against the back of his hand. An almost undetectable motion. Almost.

John's eyes follow the two ball as it touches every rail at the same point, over and over and over again, never slowing down.

Though he did not remember making plans, a wake was held. John sat at the back of the room of the funeral home and stared blankly at the coffin, his profound mania and fierce melancholy so perfectly balanced as to cancel each other out. His parents had been at his son's memorial, but their absence from Zola's was noted by all guests in their hushed conversations. John, however, saw nothing around him because there was nothing around him to see.

Zola had no family so the only mourners that showed up were Eleanor and David, some work acquaintances, a few people from Rochester, and a man that no one recognized who stayed no longer than the time it took to say a silent prayer by her coffin. When they had all gone, John sat stone-faced and alone. He held no thoughts. He heard no sounds. And just when he began to believe he were the only man alive, the funeral director approached and told him that it was time for him to go. He was a thin man in his sixties, with a brown mustache and black club master glasses and a black suit that was too big for his crumpled body. To John, he appeared to be of another species, a fish or lizard or bug that had somehow survived the flash extinction. John looked up from his chair in disbelief. The director tried to help him to his feet but when John felt the wet fin against the back of his hand, he pushed it aside, got up, and stumbled out the door.

Now he is inside of his house staring at his bed. His house has no roof. The bed is a cave hollowed out of the lake. The water around the cave is violent but inside the cavern there are soft white stars. John closes his eyes and moves through the tumbling waves. He is waist-deep in pearl foam. The pitch black of the canyon beckons to him. He submerges.

All of the pool balls come to rest at once. John buttons up his coat, adjusts his sunglasses, and walks out into the heartless storm.

When he surfaces, it will be one year later.

# CHAPTER FOUR

JOHN HAS MANY VISIONS IN HIS YEARLONG NIGHT. IN ONE OF THEM, he is seated on the couch in his home trying to remember how he got there. Only in life does John remember his dreams. In dreams, he knows nothing about his life. His beard and hair are long and unkempt and he is surrounded by clutter. There is spoiled food on the countertops, dead flowers on the table. The curtains are drawn and the television broadcasts death.

Cold War.

Propane explosion. Seven dead.

Among them, a name his dream-self recognizes. Suddenly his mother and father come through the door and John is given the feeling that he has been estranged from them for thousands of years. They sit down in chairs across from John. Somber and nervous, their eyes dart around the room in avoidance of something. Him? His mother begins to speak. The tone is angry. Turns the air to steam. John cannot understand why she would be angry at him, what he has done wrong, but her eyebrows are furrowed and the indistinguishable words she speaks are sharp and aimed at a part of him beyond his skin. The dreamer has failed them in some way, but that is not his concern.

John stares blankly at her, trying to make sense of the language, but it belongs to the space apart from them and cannot travel this far in. John's father sits back in his chair. He looks uncomfortable. Sober. John senses weakness, the worry of someone contradicting their own human nature, a pallor of dread covering the face of a man defying his instinct to flee. Out of the room. Into the bottle. But his mother is strong and purposeful, and though John cannot at first find the frequency, he knows by the inflection that she is asking a question of him. Finally, he is able to dial her in.

"What about us?"

She is asking John to remember her in this place removed from endless death.

"We lost that child too."

Major leans in, lips tight. Eyes narrow. Same long, straight sound.

"We lost that child too."

In this dream, John stands up and looks at his parents who now sit at the bottom of a great canyon, cowering and pushed firmly against the bottom of the world. John blocks out their sun. After many winters, Major stands up, rises through the atmosphere like a sudden mountain. Millennia spanned in seconds. When he is eye-to-eye with his son, they are both very old men and now their language is the same.

"The selfishness." He would know.

Astrid stands, pulling herself up light-year by light-year. There is a look of disgust on her new face.

"She never even loved you."

This note echoes for as long as John will live.

When they are gone, John walks into his bedroom and descends into the hollow.

Inside is a gray room. He is suspended above an enclosure there. The cage is rectangular in shape and there are bars designed to keep something confined. A prison with no ceiling. He notices an animal huddled in the corner staring into the middle of the prison. Its eyes are lifelessly black. It smiles but it is motionless. John reaches down with his long elastic arm and touches it. When it does not respond, he snatches the creature up and pulls it close to his face. The creature screams a high squeal then goes silent. John looks it over curiously. It is soft and bright, of no use in the kind of world at the surface. He turns the thing over and it screams again. John ignores the shrill cry. He studies it closely, its intrusive and painfully gentle dimensions. It has long ears and round body covered in blue fur. He hears a rattle from inside the beast. Not a toy's rattle. Not the playful bouncing of hollow plastic beads. This muffled clinking is more sinister. Like screws in a dryer. John turns the animal around and discovers that there is a zipper down its back. The zipper has not been closed completely. He lowers it. Inside the body there is a small orange container sealed with a white top. John looks around but sees only that outside his window there is black snow falling. He removes the container and walks into his bedroom, grabbing a bottle off the dining room table as he passes. The table is surrounded by piles of magazines and unopened letters stacked higher than ever, clumsily constructed towers that somehow have not yet toppled. The food on the counter has multiplied threefold, and it is older and the stack of dishes in the sink is wider. The petals of the flowers are now brown and scattered on the floor. How John knows this from where he sits in his dream he is not sure, but it is true. A stench permeates the air, something rotten. Decay. There are things living in the house with John now, but he has not seen them. They buzz during the day and at night they scurry. John sits down on the bed. In his right hand there is a full bottle of white pills and already he cannot remember how it got there. On the label is a name he used to speak often but now cannot pronounce. There are numbers on it, too. Dates. Doses. In his left hand is a bottle of champagne. The foil around the neck is blue.

CO344NrqetGsaRdeplATULdsflq21ATdfvjIONZ97S!

He stares at the string of random symbols. Dead language. John peels the foil back and struggles to release the cork noiselessly into the stale air. Foam boils over the top.

Her mouth.

The gorge.

Before they could turn a corner, Zola took his hand. Yes. He saw it perfectly.

John is startled by the memory that has found him here, a place he thought a sanctuary from the contagion of waking heartache. He must not be in yet. In a rush to go under, he takes a drink from the bottle at his right side and a drink from the bottle at his left. He chews the small chalky pieces harshly and tries to wash the powder down, but it congeals in multiple places between his cheek and his gums. He attempts to free the chunks of pill with his tongue and in doing so scrapes past a tooth that feels to be loose. Why? Whatever has loosened it is not yet in his memory. John knows that he still has time, that he is momentarily safe. He drinks again though from which bottle he no longer knows. Unfocused, John reaches over to the phone by the bed and dials a number. Ringing. Ringing. His spine is a liquid. Ringing. Now it is a gas. The phone drops. A woman's voice. He knows it.

John is pulled through the opening.

Awareness divides. There is he and a light and a nagging disappointment. John is in a clean bed. The room around him now is white and the flowers are in bloom. Eleanor is at the foot of the bed, looking over him, next to a machine just as tall. She looks around cautiously and then moves toward him and places a hand on his face. Her lips form shapes, but John cannot make out her words. A door opens behind her. Eleanor jumps back and John senses something terrible approaching, something large and glowing white and millions of years old. Soon it will be upon her and extinguish the radiance the room exudes. John grows fearful, triggered by the presence of the unknown object. Obscene and senseless images begin to crystalize between he and Eleanor, between Eleanor and the looming obliteration. There is a pendulum made of flesh that ticks in gruesome thuds. There is a trickle of dark blood running through a powder-white dune like a vein. When it reaches the bottom of the pale heap, it bursts into a mist against the ceiling, where it congeals and drips like tears that disappear before they land. There is a continuous loop of glass spears that appear from nothing to pierce the green petals of a flower before they vanish again. One after another after another. A clear glimmering fluid drips from the wilt. The fluid puddles on the ground and from that puddle two arms emerge with red bulbs for hands. They scramble to grip dry land before sinking back in a useless cycle of ascension and decline. John cannot comprehend any of these hallucinations, and they make his stomach turn. A pulsing machine next to him grows louder. A woman dressed in white moves Eleanor aside as she presses a series of buttons. Suddenly John is unconcerned.

His eyes are heavy, so he closes them and retreats into the calm, blank cave.

Inside is his home. The flowers are gone. The buzzing has stopped. The window near the mattress he finds himself on top of pours in heatless fire. John rolls onto his side and inhales a faint stench of bleach. His legs are pressed firmly by stiff linen tucked under the mattress that his weak body barely weighs down. There is order all around him. He lies on his back again and sighs loudly, trying to piece together a timeline that has had many moments stolen from it, many transitions between places missing from the record. Though he does not see anyone, he hears a woman's voice clearly.

"Are you awake?" It is Eleanor. She has found him in his aimless wandering through the maze of fevered sleep.

She enters his bedroom from down the hall. She is wrapped in a towel and her hair is wet. Now she sits down at his side. He is thankful for mercy here. There is the smell of shampoo wafting off of her and lotion glimmers on the taut skin of her face. Her voice is gentle but her sad eyes belie a grim anger.

"I did all I could," she says, unkindly. "But I can't stay. I'm not supposed to be here." She turns away from him and hangs in silence, breathing sharply. She opens her mouth to speak but stops herself. Then she stands and walks out. The formality lingers.

"Stay," he says. His voice is weak. An unused muscle. "Please stay."

He knows that if they are to meet again, she will have to be waiting where he washes up and there is just too much empty

space to believe the same particles will twice collide. He hears
Eleanor dressing in the bathroom. Then the back door closes.
With all the strength he has, John sits up. The room around him
is clean and in order. Books are in a row on his shelf, his clothes
are hung in the closet, his floor is clean of dust and glass and
paper. His hair too, washed and trimmed. Beard shaved. There
is a candle burning on his dresser and a cane with a shiny handle
propped up against the wall between him and the door. John uses
it to pull himself out of bed and he staggers down the hall into the
kitchen where he finds that someone has left a drink near a spot
that has been carved into the counter. Though the room is empty,
he can hear whispering in the shadows over his shoulder and feel
the weight of mournful eyes upon him. But John Harvey's focus
now is only on the end. In the cloudless tundra of searing white
sand, he has finally found it. What he doesn't know is that the end
is just as pale and hungry as he, and having arisen from beneath,
he too is now locked firmly in its sights. He too is hunted.

# CHAPTER FIVE

ZERO VISIBILITY. HAD HE NOT BEEN SO FAMILIAR WITH THE neighborhood, John would have been tumbling weightlessly through the boundless vacuum of space. He can see no traffic lights, no street signs, no building fronts. He knows that he has to make a right out the front door of the bar, walk straight until the road veers off even farther to the right, and follow the bend to the next intersection where he will find the deli immediately on the left. Even in the nastiest of blizzards, there is no way to miss the intersection, and the road he is on leads there as surely as if it were a train track. He jams his gloveless hands deep into his pockets, makes his way out to the middle of the street, and begins walking.

Considering how much it had been snowing and for how long, John fully expected to be trudging through ankle-deep piles of wet slush, but every time a flake touches down it is picked back up again and set on some new course. John is thankful for that. Then a terrible snap fills the air, sending John reeling backward in shock. He looks around, but the sound, though it was everywhere, came from nowhere and returned almost immediately to it.

*Something next. Too close.*

John covers his head and runs to the side of the road, looking back over his shoulder at the sky though there is no reason to think it came from the sky or anywhere under it. He reaches the curb and stands for a moment with one hand on his weak heart. Not thunder. Too immediate and ubiquitous without trail-off. Like being inside a rubber tube pierced by a nail. Maybe an electrical box exploded. Then, where there had not been a tree, there was a tree.

He yells and jumps back and ducks and rips off his hat and puts up his arm to guard his face and throws a punch with the hand he holds the hat in. The long, gray branches that face the sky bounce with what little life the tree has left like the expanding and contracting lungs of a dying beast. When they come to rest, John approaches it cautiously.

"Where in the hell did you come from?" he asks it.

No reply.

John knows well the streets of this neighborhood. Richmond and each residential offshoot is lined with century-old northern red oak and American sycamores with the occasional spruce in some of the larger yards where the steel magnates had built their mansions further back in the late-nineteenth century. But along the commercial streets, the oaks appear sparingly. Mostly, this is where you find the Hornbeams because they are smaller. None of the oaks John saw are as diseased as this one is, nor does he figure it would have been so close to a street as to fall across it in a mix-use district like the one he is in. A city that doesn't hesitate to cut a park in half with a highway, or to demolish an architectural masterpiece for a parking lot, would not think twice about removing a tree older than the city itself, especially if it were as sick as the one lying in front of him. John studies it closely. Without leaves, it is difficult to determine if it suffered from oak leaf blister or anthracnose, but because there are crusty black spots all over the branches and vertical stripes running down the trunk, John figures it to be hypoxylon cancer, a disease he has read about in a book published just that year called *Diseases of Trees and Shrubs* by a French botanist called Lyon.

"You almost killed me," John says, running his hand over the body of the felled titan. "I appreciate that." His finger finds the letter X carved into the trunk. He traces the man-made gouges slowly. Someone climbed very high to make such an arbitrary marking. It is then that John notices a man standing directly across from him on the other side of the tree. He calls out to the stranger who gazes past him into the static, but no sound travels and the short distance between them might as well be leagues. The man is tall like John in a jacket much like his and wearing the same hat, but unlike John his hair is short, no uncombed strands of it falling messily from beneath the knit cap. John can see that he is young, maybe in his mid- or late twenties. His face is clean-shaven and he is wearing a similar pair of, if not the exact same, sunglasses. He is also much more slender, almost sickly looking. His sharp cheekbones push against the skin of his face, and his jaw is well defined. He is leaning what little there is of his weight against the tree on his elbows. John waves his arms and screams like he is a castaway on an island and the man a distant plane, but his attempts to signal him get no response. Then there is a hand on the man's right shoulder. A woman's hand. He turns toward it and as quickly as he arrived, he is gone. Vanished completely into the blizzard.

Again, John calls out, but his voice crumbles at his feet. He leaps over the tree trunk and runs blindly toward the inner layers of the storm, screaming after the apparition until he can't run anymore. His lungs tired, his blood hot, John bends over and clutches his thighs, and as he desperately tries to catch his breath, he looks around the fallen sky and knows something is wrong. The road should have veered by now. And even if somehow the tree had fallen behind him and not directly in front, he would have walked past the bar again. Instead there is only a straight road at his feet both in front of him and behind. No discernible buildings, no signs, no indication he is even in that same city anymore let alone on that road. He is neither present nor lost yet both. The only thing he can do is keep walking, trusting that whatever path he's on will bring him back to a place he once knew.

*You either go or you don't.*

John soon reaches the lake. Gigantic patches of ice sway across dark water, groaning and creaking as they collide. John finds himself standing against the guardrail that stretches for a few hundred yards in both directions and watches as the crystal islands move gracelessly like chess pieces in front of a crude giant. John finally knows exactly where he is. He takes a moment to remember the vision, to bring the awareness back to it that once made it real but could never quite awaken it into truth. Behind him there will be a bench. Black. Curved back. Steel. Next to the bench, a tree. He had been there when he was young and should have been there growing old. John turns and it is just as he thought. The emerald leaves of a familiar tree rustle noisily above it, stroked by a soft hand. Underneath, the blades of the ankle-high grass lean back with the breeze. John can smell it through the cold, and it reminds him of his life before the black door closed behind him, when he could withdraw from the world to see love like a dream, the imprint of timeless perfection left with a single mystifying touch. He had that once, but it did not accompany him through. John takes off his coat and sits down.

With his hand on the small of her back, John guided Zola up the stairs. The door at the top was black. He opened it and ushered her inside. There was a herd of animals seated at a table. Their food had been ravaged, their cups were tipped over and empty. Zola walked over to the jukebox and made a selection. "The Gates of Delirium" began to play. She took the seat they had saved for her. Then she and the animals howled madly.

There is a shape rising out of the dark water. It lurches up and falls back against a slab of ice and then slides into the lake out of sight. After a few seconds, the water's current causes whatever it is to repeat these three very precise motions until John is sure of what he is looking at: a body. He stands up from the bench and walks hurriedly over to the rail. Leaning out beyond it to get a better look only confirms that there is a woman in a dress riding the pale horse of the frozen tide. Though he knows there is no chance of her being alive in those temperatures, John climbs over the railing anyway and carefully makes his way down the slippery rocks that line the shore; huge rocks between which old scraps of clothing had collected along with the bones of fish and birds. The fresh water of the lake slams against them and leaps into the air where the droplets instantly turn to ice and fall back into themselves, the sound like a sheet of hail pummeling tin.

The body floats nearer. John cannot reach it alone but knows that with a long enough stick, he might be able to twist it up in the ends of her dress and pull her in. She is facedown and her hair sways violently, itself a livid storm that rages without purpose. Her arms float up at the sides of her head, like she is flying above all that cold darkness looking down. John finds a piece of driftwood and gets as close to the edge of the rocks as he can. He clumsily thumps it against her back but manages to make a pulling motion as he does. She comes closer. With her feet the farthest thing away from him, John can't get a good angle with which to dredge her out, so he sticks the end of the piece of wood into the nest of hair and twists. Bracing his foot against a crack in the stone, he starts to pull. The body breaches with a formidable ease. When she is finally out of the water and slumped on a wet rock, John leans back, soaking and breathless. He thinks for a second of turning her over, but he already knows by the green dress and the way her hair is beautifully tangled around the stick like a hairpin that the body had once belonged to Zola.

John returns to the bench under the tree and Zola sits next to him. They both look quietly in the direction of the invisible lake, a scene built by an architect either too eager to please or not eager enough.

"Why are you here?" he asks her.

"I don't know. I didn't mean to be. Suddenly, I just was."

"Do you miss me?"

Zola answers him in a voice as lacking in kindness as he remembered it being. "I miss certain things. Things you did. Maybe they weren't you. Who knows? I didn't care. They pleased me."

"I waited to call an ambulance," he says. "Don't be mad. Everything was lost anyway. No need to come back to this place."

"I don't know what this place is."

John looks around into the caverns of white that lie just beyond the fresh grass and scratches his beard. "Yeah, me neither."

"But thank you…" She pauses, tries to remember. "John. John something." Zola stands up and moves to the edge of the grass where the blizzard began.

"John something," he says after her.

Zola looks out at the lake that brought her in.

"You won't see what's not in front of you," he calls out. "Not in a storm like this."

"Someone else is here."

He gets up and stands next to her at the front. On the walkway that runs parallel to the lake looking out over the roiling water is the Woman in White.

"Oh. Her. Yeah. She's local."

"Is she lost?" Zola asks.

"Definitely not."

"I've never seen her before."

"She didn't appear until you went away."

"But still." Zola and John sit back down together, closer this time but still not close enough to touch. "Is there anything else?"

John thinks for a moment. "What happens after you die?"

Zola shrugs, bored. "Mostly the same things that happen after you're born. But without any surprise."

"That must be nice." John doesn't mean to do it, but he looks at her belly.

"Knowing doesn't change anything. Seeing it coming doesn't stop it from coming."

He nods.

"Can I ask you a question now?" Zola says.

"Okay."

"What happened to you after I left? I lost sight of you."

"I'm not sure. I don't remember much. But when I came back, everything was different."

Zola bows her head and touches the place on her finger where her wedding ring once was or where it eventually would be. "I put the third bottle of pills where it could find only you. When you were ready for it."

"Thank you. Unfortunately, they didn't work."

"No?"

He laughs. "No. Life is the *only* thing I have left in me."

Another pause. John readies himself to leap across an enormous depth.

"Ask me what you really want to know," Zola says.

"Was he mine?"

The distant lake wore the evening haze like a robe. John was nine and sitting on a park bench in between the muted late-August sun and his mother, who was looking out toward the horizon. Her long hair blew as she breathed the saltless wet air in through her nose. It was summer, but the clouds were already busy pulling their shadows in, setting up the autumn palate of color. John was counting the waves when he noticed a bleached white stick protruding from a rock not more than halfway between where he sat and the edge of the water. He stood up and took a few steps away toward it.

"Be careful," Astrid said, then smiled and again went back through a door that opened only when her eyes were not. There was no guardrail yet so if you had the courage to traverse the field of wet boulders, which John did, you could wade out as far as you wanted. He stepped carefully—he was small, and his feet were nimble. When he reached the stick protruding from between two flat stones, he found that it was smoother and whiter than any beach wood he had seen. John grabbed it and tried to pull it free, but it wouldn't budge. It was attached to something below the surface.

John looked down. A deer, upturned and stuck. Not long dead. Maggots were still eating its face. Terrified, he looked up and saw that beyond it, between it and the sun, a formless unlit space emerged from the water that spread up and out, pushing aside the sky and everything in it, not just impassable but inescapable now that John had seen what was down there.

Zola's voice moves through him in spasms as John falls short of the ledge and into a sleepless void. The smooth glory of doubt ravaged by one word that pulls him helplessly through the turns of a labyrinth toward a center of unending noise. When John closes his eyes, he sees the animal's sun-bleached tongue hanging from its mouth. It looks human.

John's eyes were full of tears, but he couldn't scream because what he was experiencing was so much worse than fear.

One day it would be called something specific, but he does not know that word yet.

Driven mad by curiosity, desperate for a foothold in his experience, some similar shape to compare to this nameless expression of life, he peered down again. Exposed ribs around a rotting earthbound heart. Abandoned pink intestines writhing with insect life and larva. The nothing directly under the all. The empty adjacent to the full. There was nowhere John could go where death was not already there waiting.

He returns to the bench next to the memory that moors an exhausted woman.

"No."

Sun blisters in John's muscles.

"He wasn't."

Sun blisters in John's bones.

"You knew that, John," Zola says. "You never saw us all at once."

Though he knows they have not been there, John enters through the soot-covered doorframe of his apartment. A flame was here, but it too could not stay. He picks up a charred pile of papers and begins to thumb carefully through them. Old wants, stacked both above him to the ceiling and below him through the floor. Post-it notes.

*stairwell. south side of building 53. 11:45am.*

The handwriting is familiar, but the name is gone. John moves on throughout the home reading the unopened longings that littered every burnt surface. He digs through the filth that has accumulated, the dishes, the discarded, the dead things. He looks down into the broken glass of the mirror. He opens the cupboards and drawers and even peers into the crater where the signal of his father still echoes around the unused machinery of creation, changing direction at its boundaries but never losing strength. Nothing. And when he is convinced he has overturned every other stone on his abandoned earth, he cautiously removes the last brick from a crumbling wall and opens the box where he hides his shame. He pushes aside the letter and rummages through all the memories he has pulled from time. Not one of them shows his family together. Not one of those memories is his own.

"No. I didn't."

"So how does someone expect what they cannot even imagine?"

John gazed drearily into the orange and saw more pills. Not sure how many. Ten, maybe. But he was already dizzy and the walls around him were falling away into a kaleidoscopic mosaic. The ringing in his ears was thick as syrup. His stomach turned. His eyelids got heavy. He let the bottle drop and the pills he would have needed to go in after them rolled under the bed. He heard them falling like rain before coming to rest. Then he went to sleep, but not for good. There was a far-off voice calling his name in something like a panic.

A white cold wave crashes against the break wall a hundred yards off the shore. Zola looks up.

"I have to go now," she says.

John reaches out and tries to touch her hand, but she moves it away. "When did you stop loving me?" he asks.

"I don't remember."

"Will I find you again?"

"I don't think so. There is too much space. Goodbye…" Zola struggles to find what comes next.

"John," he says.

"Goodbye, John."

Without a kiss, without contact, Zola walks to the edge. Then she climbs over the railing and is gone, lost to him like numbers in a dream. John is cold again.

# CHAPTER SIX

Having traveled as far as the lake meant all John can do now is turn around and go back. There is nothing beyond that rail, but he knows that if he keeps the water behind him and doesn't make any sudden turns, he can follow Transit Road from its peak all the way into the city (beyond it, even into the suburbs, if he wanted to), where he will eventually come upon the road that will take him home. He takes a last look at the bench covered in a film of snow, its backrest warped from years of applied pressure, and understands that it is exactly how it should have looked from the beginning. Empty. It had to be to finally come into view.

The sun was bright, and the air was warm for October. The bus stop was exactly eight minutes away from the grocery store on foot and he knew he had at least thirteen to catch the 23 to Filmore, but John couldn't afford to be late. Zola would be up from her nap soon if she wasn't already, and being six months pregnant meant simple tasks were getting harder without his help. She would be expecting lunch.

John found himself in a swarm of old women shuffling away from St. Mary's Church after service let out as he passed it on the way to his stop. Eventually he was able to defect as it moved beyond the enclosed bus shelter, and when it departed without him, he discovered a woman left behind, sitting alone on the bench. He didn't know for sure if she was part of the same undulating, geriatric herd or if she had just materialized without his noticing, but he recognized her from his neighborhood. Her name was Opal. She lived seven houses down from him. They had never spoken but because they were the only two people at the stop they smiled politely as John took a seat along the same blue bench.

Opal and her husband Silas were churchgoers who retired from teaching to start a nonprofit community-service organization that kept the city's homeless warmly clothed in the winter. But now, a widow in her late fifties, the once prominent member of the community was rarely seen. That afternoon, her long silver hair was pulled back off her forehead with a headband and went down to nape of her neck. She wore a high-cut yellow dress with a white floral pattern and a gold necklace with a low-hanging cross. The wrinkles in the fair skin of her face were shallow and few but well earned. Silas had died from a cerebral aneurysm in church a few months after beginning their charity work. Though she and John never shared more than a distant wave, which was becoming less and less frequent as time passed, he knew her story. Buffalo was small, and news spread quickly, particularly if that news was unfortunate.

According to some men at the bar who knew some women who had some friends who claim to have been there, Silas started to slur his speech during the Eucharistic Prayer on a bleak Sunday morning. Embarrassed, Opal nudged him with her elbow and admonished him through clenched teeth, but her anger became concern when Silas turned to look at her and she could see in his eyes that he did not understand why the words were coming out that way, all "jumbled up and slow-like." He pawed at his mouth and jaw and looked fearfully around a church he didn't recognize while sounds he didn't choose fell from his trembling lips. As the prayer ended and everyone sat back down, Silas fell over.

John does not know how long he has been walking, but he makes no turns and sees nothing familiar. His legs are tired, and his cheeks are so cold they burn.

The story goes that when Silas lost consciousness, Opal surrendered to the dread completely. Anguished screams. Parishioners now leaping into action. Some pulled him into the aisle and began CPR. Others stood and clutched their pearls, fanned their faces, aghast, hands over their mouths, stretching their necks to see better. An ambulance was called but Silas was gone by the time paramedics arrived.

Some say that as Opal lay hunched over him calling out to God in deep, woeful sobs, there was a wind that snuffed out each candle on the votive stand near the altar though no doors or windows had been open that day. Others say that ain't true but did swear that in his moments spent disconnected, Silas was actually prophesying, not just stammering, and they used his fit as proof of the power of the word of God himself, so overwhelming and incomprehensible that if He chooses you as His mouthpiece you are forever altered by the divine encounter. But what exactly Silas said, if he said anything at all, had gotten so distilled passing through the experiences and preferences of the meddling locals that Silas the man had essentially vanished in order that his message survive and be allowed to mutate into whatever form faith required of it. Depending on what point the storyteller was trying to drive home and how much they'd had to drink when telling it, John had heard accounts ranging from "he warned that man's final hour is upon us" to "he assured a Sabres Stanley Cup victory by 1997." A man who spent his life devoted to goodness had been reduced to a decaying signal inside an iron box of a city.

But Opal Pike was seen by locals as a holy relic, a woman separated from the sacred by a mere one degree, because she had been married to the man chosen to speak the word.

"Juss like Moses!" proclaimed Ralph, the very first time he told John the story of Silas Pike. "An' han' ta Gahd, I shit you not, he says we're gettin' an AM&A's inna plaza by my house."

"Oh come on. That's such bullshit," John remonstrated.

"The things you drunk lunatics make real to silence your own madness would put the Creator himself to shame," Bertie said, eavesdropping on the conversation from a few stools down.

"HAN' TA FRICKIN' GAHD!" Ralph screamed at him.

John sees a vague shape in distance. Someone is walking directly toward him. John's muscles tense. Animal-like, the hair on his arms stands up straight and his eyes narrow. The man approaching him is wearing a jacket like his and his hair is long and black. He has a beard too and appears to be wearing sunglasses. His posture, his very presence out here in the storm, and the speed with which he walks directly toward him strike John as threatening. Though John's hands are cold, he knows he can throw them quickly if need be.

Those brave or shameless enough to ignore social graces interrogated Opal about Silas's habits while alive, venerating her as some kind of living saint. They fawned over his memory, treating his absence like the presence of a celebrity. But it was obvious to John, who only saw her from a distance, that this made her uncomfortable. Because what John also sensed was that Opal was made human by her suffering. To him, it did not exalt her as it might to others, but instead brought her closer to the world. And the more often she left her house to return to that church, to that place of death and uncertainty, the further she seemed from anything supernatural.

It is not until they are a few feet away from each other that John realizes he has been approaching his own reflection in a pane of glass of a bus stop shelter.

When Opal again looked to him and greeted him with half a nod, John noticed something about her that he had not seen in anyone before. She had different-colored eyes. The left one a lush green; her right eye a deep, coffee brown.

"Wow," he said.

"Excuse me?"

"Heterochromia. I've only seen it in animals."

Opal seemed offended, and rightfully so.

"No, not like that. I'm sorry. I work with film and probably know a little too much about color processing."

She responded with a dismissive "mmhmm" under her breath.

"I'm really sorry."

Opal glared at him for a moment, sizing him up. Then, "I will admit, the fact that you know the term is impressive. Most people just tell me I got dogs' eyes."

"Yeah?" John asked, excitedly. "Then you're going to be blown away when I tell you about the differences in chemical developer between the C-41 and the RA-4 process." Opal didn't laugh. "My name is John Harvey," he continued. "We live in the same neighborhood."

"Hi. Yes, I know." She reluctantly put out her hand. "I used to see you watching me prune my garden. Opal Pike."

"Oh. Yeah. I was admiring your Knapp Hills."

She clutched her purse. "My what?"

"Your azaleas."

John sits inside the glass booth and lights a cigarette. He knows no bus will arrive, but he needs a break from the whipping wind. His legs are unusually tired. Bones sore and flimsy, thigh muscles burning like he had been running for days. Beside him on the inside of the glass is an advertisement that he immediately recognizes.

They sat in silence for a long time. Then, to his surprise, Opal spoke. "I really hate this thing," she said, referring to the advertisement for a Kelsey-Hayes Prefab Fallout Shelter that hung on the inside of the glass wall. "I wish they would take it down already."

John squinted and leaned in to note the details of the poster. In it, a family of four relaxed inside of a box with thick black borders impervious to a bright red world outside of them that had reduced their home to a few charred support beams. A chill came over him. Not exactly déjà vu but close to it. "It is a little weird that these people would be so calm while the world is on fire."

Opal squared her shoulders and straightened her back. "I am referring to the concept in general." Her tone was austere.

"A fallout shelter is unnatural. It's not the will of God. That we as a culture should advertise such immorality is a disgrace." She turned away from John and shook her head in disgust.

John didn't agree, but in the face of the horrible silence he had just come from, he decided to engage her. "What do you mean unnatural?"

"What I mean is that when you exclude yourself from the world, you are removed from the light of God. By hiding underground in one of these," she moved her hand over the ad, "bunkers? You are refusing to acknowledge the plan that the Lord has set for you. Faking death to fool life is dishonest."

John pretended to weigh her perspective and though he knew it directly conflicted with Post's ideals of etiquette, he ventured to be clever. "Don't you think that sometimes it's just what it takes to survive? You're told to play dead in a bear attack, too. I wouldn't necessarily consider that to be sinful. You know? Just…necessary."

Opal tightened her lips. "Hiding away until pain passes is not surviving, Mr. Harvey." Her eyes shimmered. "Living through that pain is. You should not be able to return to this world if you have tricked it into sparing you. That is not what God intended."

"Okay," John said, somewhat conceding. "But let's pretend I am considering buying one of these things because I'm a wealthy, pipe-smoking American, like this guy here, and I want to take my family underground if and when Russia finally decides to press the button. On my way to the hatch with my wife and my kid, I see you ready to go down with the ship and I ask you to join us."

"No. Life is up here. On the surface. Life is weathering those storms."

"So you would refuse?"

"Indeed, I would."

"That stubbornness could get you killed."

"This stubbornness is what keeps me alive, Mr. Harvey." She said it so angrily that John felt it on his skin. "And I would add that if you go away, you'd better stay away. This world is for us survivors. It is not yours." She shook her head and looked him in the eyes. "No. It is not yours."

Those words.

The bus arrived. Opal got up from her seat, but John did not. There was an echo in his head and as long it repeats, he cannot move.

"Are you coming?"

"I don't think so," he said quietly. "There will be another one."

"Do not take that for granted, John. See you soon." Opal climbed aboard and the bus pulled away.

John puts out his cigarette, stands up from the bench, and emerges from the glass refuge into a desert of snow.

# CHAPTER SEVEN

A BLACK SEDAN GOING FIVE MILES AN HOUR APPROACHES JOHN from behind as it lurches through the storm, and since no light travels from the high-beams, it is only the sound of the windshield wipers that alerts him to the car's proximity. John moves quickly off to the side of the road, but as he stands there waiting for it to pass, another car appears seemingly out of nowhere. Then another. Then another and another, sedans materializing from the void of snow and disappearing into it again. He notices that each has a small orange flag attached to its antenna. A funeral procession.

When the strange loop finally comes to an end, John falls into line a few paces behind the last car. He figures he can use the procession like a gulf stream current, riding it to a place that might have a phone so that he can call a cab and give the driver a location for the first time all day. He walks along behind the rearmost vehicle in the motorcade, listening intently to the windshield wipers, the intermittent woeful moan his north star, guiding him toward someone's grave. John has never been to a funeral before, let alone a funeral in the snow. His unborn son had been given a service by the hospital and cremated. Zola too.

Their ashes in boxes somewhere under clutter. Just wood and embers. Things left behind by a fire. Not by a wife. Not by a child.

John wonders if they have broken ground today in this storm or if they had already dug a winter's worth of holes in anticipation of things like this. Weather like this. Months ago, in the sun, digging the graves for people who didn't need them yet. Just in case. The drawn scream of the windshield wipers begins to grow louder with each slow and futile pass across the glass. Just in case some guy's cancer gets a second wind. Louder. In case a missing person is found near the river. Deafening now. In case an old woman's car is pushed through an intersection and into oncoming traffic. John cannot ignore the piercing screech of the windshield wipers. He covers his ears but the sound isn't only around him, it is inside of him. It vibrates every atom, urging John inward. Frequency increasing. Length of the waves shorter. Shorter. A focal point. The driver's seat of his car.

It is early in March of 1983 and it is raining. John's Buick Skylark is stopped along the curb in front of Brinks, where the neon of the sign above the door leaks in through the passenger window and drapes itself over Eleanor's back like a shawl. She is hunched over in the seat next to John with her head in her hands. On the phone she had been crying. Words slurred, she'd told him she needed a ride home. John figured she was just drunk and being overly sentimental, but when she steps into his car he sees that she is upset, shaken, and he is embarrassed that the thought of meeting her alone had excited him. He wants to get away from where they are parked as soon as possible in case either of them is recognized. He knows how it might look and, unfortunately for him, it isn't what it seems.

John puts the car in drive and moves up the street, veering around the bend and down Augustine Avenue for a few blocks before hitting a red light. Eleanor still has her face buried in her hands, weeping. The radio is off. John grips the wheel and he leans forward to look up into the sky, trying to find a constellation hidden in the thunderstorm, a cloud pattern, anything to distract himself from thinking about Eleanor naked while she is in such obvious crisis. It doesn't work. He sits back. The light has been red for too long. The windshield wipers fail to cast off the curtain of rain that hides them from the searchlight moon. For now, John and Eleanor are alone, and their absence is unnoticed. At home, Zola is passed out on the couch. There is an empty bottle of Bully Hill wine on the table in front of her and she is wearing an oversized, white T-shirt and shorts and the TV is on. John knows this because it is the last thing he saw when he looked in to make sure she was sleeping before sneaking out the back door. The clock on the radio says 11:38 p.m.

Eleanor takes a deep breath and sits up straight.

"You okay?" John asks.

"I am not."

"Why did you call my house this late? What if Zola had answered?"

"Then I would have asked *her* to come get me. You just happened to pick up the phone first. I'm sorry. I had no one else to call."

The light turns green.

"So what happened?"

"He's cheating on me."

John shrugs. "You guys cheat on each other. That's what you do."

"Don't be an asshole, John. That's only sex. His heart is with someone else. I know it."

Eleanor had told John this very same thing before. Monday, December 14, 1981. Zola had led him and Eleanor and David on an adult field trip through the Albright-Knox Art Gallery, which she had been trying to visit since she moved in with John. Eleanor and John were standing in front of Pollock's *Convergence*, looking intensely for the match embedded in the paint, while Zola and David had gone on ahead to escape the scrutinizing eye of the security guard and sip from the flask Zola had snuck in. Eleanor waited until they turned a corner. When she was certain David was out of earshot, she turned to John and said, "His heart sees someone else."

John gave up trying to find the match and stepped back. "What do you mean?"

"I mean I think he's dating someone," she responded. "Like, not just fucking. Falling in love."

A couple at the Gorky beside the obese guard looked back over their shoulders at Eleanor in disgust. The thin, stuffy, older man put his arm around the waist of the woman next to him and moved her farther down the hall.

Very quietly, John said, "How do you know?"

Eleanor too stepped back from the painting and stood shoulder to shoulder with John. As she tilted her head and moved her eyes over its entirety, she replied, "He called me 'Beth' when I was sucking his dick."

The woman flashed Eleanor a look and snapped the back of her teeth with her tongue.

"Sorry," Eleanor said to her. *"Penis."*

Eleanor reaches into her long brown coat and pulls out an envelope.

"I found a letter."

*Change the name at the bottom. Please. It's not too late. The letter is still in the envelope. I'll never know anyone or anything interfered. Please just change the signature. Please. It doesn't have to be.*

Eleanor takes the letter out and unfolds it. John tries to keep his eyes on the road, but in his periphery he sees the way the T is crossed. The way a L is looped. Not exact, but possibly familiar. The rain doesn't just fall now; it undulates against the car. The entire night melts around him.

"It was in the mailbox. In a woman's handwriting and addressed only to David with no return. Journalistic instinct says, 'that's a story.' I shouldn't have opened it. But I did. And now there's no putting it back."

"Who is it from?"

Eleanor stares silently at the letter in her lap. An eternity passes. "I don't know. This slut signed it using some cutesy fucking nickname. But I think I have an idea."

John looks over at the letter, scanning it quickly at first but eventually letting his eyes linger on certain letters, then on words, then finally on phrases, cutting the pain into incrementally larger doses, the road ahead left unwatched. The creases in the paper are deep and many. It was meant to be tucked away and found later. Shoved into a palm under the surface level of a conversation or stashed away in a coat pocket with a subtle wink. But it wasn't exchanged personally. It was mailed. Whoever wrote it had failed to hand it off. Had doubt set in? Had fear?

John entered his cubicle and sat down at his desk on the morning of Monday, July 14. A Post-it note was stuck to the handle of the top drawer. It was the first time he had ever seen Zola's handwriting. Sharp cursive, leaning right and riotous. He thought about the hand that crafted it, the way it looked in his own hand two nights before. Meek but not delicate, a dark-red nail polish adorning the fingers that inched closer along the top of the bar until finally one of them met his, fingers that would be clumsily undoing the pearl snaps of his plaid shirt and prying apart the buckle of his leather belt a few hours later in a port-a-potty outside of the Yes concert at Rich Stadium.

"Is he fucking her?" John asks. It isn't exactly what he wants to know but it's as close as he can get.

Eleanor laughs and brushes a wet, curly lock of brown hair away from her eye. "Of course," she says. "If it is who I think it is, we *both* did. That's what we do."

John resents her candor.

"But this is love," says Eleanor. That word—*love*—leaves her mouth like campfire smoke. "Whoever this is, she's in love with my husband. And he is in love with her."

Eleanor starts crying again. John had never imagined her being so lovesick. The crosscurrent of her soft being and harsh tone makes John unsteady. He wants to comfort her and at the same time rebuke her for leading with her heart.

He decides instead to say nothing.

"That has never been part of our deal," she says. "No feelings. If I let him have others there would never be love. He promised me. No love."

John's mind finds its way back to the letter in her hand. Post-it notes. A time and a place. Usually a utility closet but occasionally a lesser-used stairwell or the back seat of the very same car he was now driving toward a red light at the corner of Augustine and Forest Avenue.

The first car of the funeral procession makes its turn into a cemetery. He has kept every single one of those notes. Useless data somewhere in the disarray still clinging to shrapnel.

John waited on a Saturday afternoon for the 3:30 from Rochester. When it pulled in, he watched through the large windows as Zola Lumi stepped off the Trentway-Wager talking with someone she had befriended on the ride—an older man who touched her elbow as he parted, walking along the outside of the building toward the cabs in the street, looking back over his shoulder at her repeatedly. Unfamiliar with the station, Zola did not notice John sitting there when she came into the lobby, which gave him a few seconds to see her as she truly was. The inextinguishable spirit of nature itself, untamable and pure. Curious and all-knowing, breathtaking, poised amidst the drastic change of shifting phases, standing valiant in the bus station of new city awaiting a stranger like she were returning home to family. Intimately familiar with the unexpected. He thought Zola was rushing water of a woman.

She wore black jeans, white Converse high-tops, and an unzipped green hoodie with a thin white V-neck T-shirt over a black lace bra, her long brown hair carelessly twisted up in a bun as it normally was at work. Without makeup, as she was that afternoon, Zola seemed divine. John could not believe she was there for him;

a soft-spoken, slightly obese, awkward and anxious virgin who had never been on a date, never traveled outside the city, considered his mother his only friend, never danced, never got drunk, never let go. He knew it was just a matter of time before she determined John Harvey's estimated worth had been severely miscalculated and reverted back to an occasional closed-mouth smile at work, but until then he would surrender to the thoughts and desires and memories of the dreamer that had placed him firmly without will in the middle of this illusion. A simulation so perfect it breathed his air.

Zola dropped her small bag at her side, stretched her arms, and yawned. It was then that she saw John watching her and, playfully embarrassed, covered up the part of her belly she had accidentally exposed. She zipped her hooded sweatshirt and flung the strap of a canvas bag over her shoulder. The light facing the perpendicular Forest Avenue is still green and John has not begun to slow the car down. He stood up from the plastic seat and tried hard to get the grin off of his face, but it was permanently affixed. The third car in the procession passes through the cemetery gates.

"You're actually here!" she said, approaching him with a small, lively skip. "I was worried you might get cold feet."

John pointed to a dangerous-looking man near the vending machines wearing a Buffalo Bills parka. "Oh, I was just here buying some crack. I forgot you were even coming."

Zola smiled and reached up to wrap her arms around his thick neck. He could feel her eyes close against his chest, her whole body slowly, softly blinking.

It was real.

"You smell musky but delicate," he said. John took his arms from around her and stepped back.

"Shit," Zola exclaimed, grabbing her T-shirt at the collar and inhaling. "New perfume. I was going for horny and desperate. Good thing I saved the receipt. You ready to get out of here? I need a drink."

John reached into his pockets. "I have some change for the vending machine if you need it."

Zola looked at him incredulously. When she decided he was joking, she threw her head back and emitted a disproportionate amount of laughter.

John, of course, was not joking, but he went with it to save face.

"Do you need to freshen up at my place or anything?" Having only recently moved out of his parents' cramped basement and into his first apartment, John was as excited at the amount of space as he was at the prospect of a guest that might actually be impressed by his record collection or the autographed glossy of Jim Kelly he won in a raffle at a coworker's stag party. Winning that coveted prize made him popular that night, and he figured it's what Jim Kelly must have felt like all the time. He regretted not taking advantage of his size in high school by playing football, but that would have required a father who taught him skills beyond flipping a zippo lighter closed or how to cheat when keeping score at bowling.

"John, we're going to drink at like three forty-five in the afternoon and then to a concert. Do you think I give a shit how I look? No matter what I do today, you're going to believe it's perfect. It's the *only* day I have that working to my advantage."

"I'm sorry," he said. "I'm nervous."

"Awww, that's adorable!" She put her arm around his waist and her head on his shoulder. John felt his genitals twitch.

"Don't be nervous, John something. I'm the same girl you see at work every day, except tonight there's a chance I'll be naked." When they twitched again, John knew he must be in love.

Not much of a drinker, John took Zola to the only bar he is even remotely familiar with, a dimly lit dive near his new place called "Brinks." Cheap drinks, pool table, patio in the summer, grill behind the bar making greasy bologna sandwiches, stacked jukebox. There they met another couple that had recently moved to Buffalo from Cleveland. Eleanor and David. Eleanor had been an editor at a liberal, independent newspaper with its headquarters in a small office in the heart of the city, but when she got a job offer from *The Buffalo News,* she packed up and moved. David followed. She was surprisingly tall, almost as tall as John, and thin. She wore large glasses with pink, plastic frames. Her skin was fair and her lips were full. That afternoon she had on a white tank top tucked into denim shorts. She had no bra on. Her breasts were firm but small. The bangs of her shoulder-length, wavy brown hair stopped just above her huge hazel eyes. Her hands were always in her pockets and she smiled a lot. David was muscular but shorter than John. His brown hair was long and feathered and his beard was carefully trimmed. He wore an oversized, white button-down shirt with the top three buttons undone. His chest was hairy. There was a gold cross dangling from his left ear. To no one's surprise, he sold car stereos.

After a few drinks, Eleanor and Zola branched off into their own conversation, leaving John to make small talk with David.

"You like music?" David asked.

"Yeah, sure," John said. "You?"

"Oh, of course. Of course. Yeah. Way into it. *Big* time."

"Oh. So, who do you like? Who is your favorite?"

David laughed and stroked his chin. "Who do I like? Let's see, oh, I don't know, gee, maybe Kenny Loggins!?" David spread his arms wide, presenting himself as the personified version of the entire Loggins mythology.

John suppressed his instinct to laugh. "I don't—is that a group?"

"Might as well be. One of the most powerful singers I've ever heard. Got the range of ten men in his golden pipes."

"Oh. I don't know him too well," John said. He was lying.

David was incredulous. "You don't know Kenneth Clark Loggins? You've got to be fucking kidding me."

"No, sorry," John lied again. "Never heard of them."

"IT'S ONE MAN!" David yelled. John flinched and realized that messing with David might be more dangerous than he thought. When the girls looked over, David apologized and collected himself. "I'm sorry. It's one man. His name is Kenny Loggins."

John bit his lip and pressed on. "What song is he famous for? Maybe I'll recognize it."

"Junkanoo Holiday?"

John shook his head.

"House at Pooh Corner?"

Again.

"Are you fucking serious?"

"Sorry, Dave. Not ringing a bell."

David looked around the room in disbelief and quietly muttered "this fucking guy" to himself.

"What's that?" John asked.

"I said it's your loss, man. That's the real shit right there. Real music. Not this BS you and your old lady listen to.

Where'd you say you were going? The Yes concert? Probably should be called NO, if you ask me."

John was a little surprised that David knew their music well enough to even have an opinion.

"Oh, you've listened to them before?"

"No, I have not. That's why I said 'probably.'"

The conversation abruptly ended. John looked at the ceiling in silence. Finally, David announced that he was "gonna go powder his nose." He tapped his nostril and turned around, and before he had taken a single step toward the bathroom, John fled the spot. As he approached the two women, they stopped talking and giggled. It made him nervous.

"What is so funny? Why are you guys laughing at me?"

"Jesus, John, we're not laughing at you," Eleanor said. "Settle down. You just make us smile!"

He apologized for overreacting. Said it was a habit he'd been trying hard to break.

David returned from the bathroom and stood at Eleanor's side, sniffing wildly and running his hand through his floppy hair. Then he whispered something in her ear. John noticed Zola bite her straw as she took a sip of her drink, her eyes fixated on the salesman—the dopey guy with the luxurious beard and the gold jewelry that would probably get mistaken for a cop if he didn't perpetually have cocaine in his mustache. As David spoke to her privately, Eleanor smirked and glanced at Zola, then made eye contact with John and laughed. John again felt diminished and removed. Reaching over the bar, Eleanor grabbed a pen and wrote her number down on a napkin and handed it to Zola. She told John they should all get together again sometime soon, but looked only at Zola while saying it. David kissed the back of Zola's hand before pulling John in for a hug with two enormous pats on the back. He told John he'd let him borrow his Loggins tape next time they saw each other, and John feigned excitement. When they left, Zola sat in the place David once did with her back to the door. Eleanor looked back over her shoulder and waved. Nobody knew that but she and John.

"Miss me?" Zola asked before loudly slurping what remained of her drink.

John could not think to be playful with the heat waves of insecurity crashing over him. "Sure."

"Oh, this is the serious John? I got the serious version now?"

John ignored her. "Should we get going? We need to stay on schedule if we want to get everything done."

"No! Bring the other John back," Zola whined. "I don't like serious John. Have fun with *meeee*." She tugged hard on the front of his shirt. "Don't worry about the time. We're fine." She flagged down the bartender. "What else do you even want to do? I thought we were gonna get drunk and then go see a band and then go back to your place and hook up. I'm not trying to take a historical tour of the city here."

The bartender hobbled over. He was even bigger than John, a gigantic, bald, pockmarked, and red-faced man who could not breathe without wheezing. When he spoke, it sounded like his vocal cords had been replaced by two old ropes vibrating in a bed of pebbles.

"Another one, babe?" he growled as he hiked up his sagging jeans.

"Yes please, Matty," Zola said.

"John, you good?" Matty barked.

Zola shook her head vigorously. "No, he is not! He's way too sober still. Get him a Thorogood, please. Dealer's choice."

"Goddammit, I just left that side of the bar, you're gonna make me walk right back there? Tryna give me a friggin' heart attack?"

"Pleeeeeease, Matty?"

Matty took a deep, strained breath and bravely started his journey of seven feet.

"So you and Matty are close now, huh?"

"What can I say—I'm likable. You'd better snatch me up quick while you can."

"Oh?"

"Yup," Zola said proudly.

John snickered. "So what was going on with you and Eleanor? Were you guys talking about me or something?"

"No!"

"You were. I know it. What were you saying?" John's voice was shaking. He scratched at his beard.

The entire day had gone by and nobody told him. Not another student, not a teacher, no one—they just smiled as he approached and laughed as he moved by. It was his mother who finally removed the paper taped to his back when he got off the bus. With tears in her eyes, she crumpled it up and threw it away. She would not let him see what it said.

"I swear we were not. Okay. I'll tell you, but don't tell them I told you."

"Fine."

"They swing. They're swingers."

"As in they're professional dancers?"

Zola laughed. "You're too much. No. You know…" She leaned in and whispered, "They fuck other people together."

John's ingenuous heart began to ache at the thought.

"I knew there was something creepy about them."

Zola shrugged. "Don't judge."

"Sorry." There was an extended pause, and in it John found the courage to take his shot. Being that he was about to make the first reference to the act of sexual intercourse in his entire life, he knew that their future, if any, hinged on what would come after.

"So…did they ask us?"

Zola smirked. "There's an *us*?"

Wheezing horribly, Matty put one bourbon, one scotch, and one beer on the bar in front of John, then grabbed the pine with two hands and hung his head to catch his breath. The very presence of the shot glasses filled John with dread.

"Let's dance," Zola said, pushing them toward him.

John put back the bourbon and scotch without hesitating and chased them so quickly that the beer foamed out of the bottle and down his chin. He coughed and wiped the tears from his eyes.

"Okay, now we can go," she said, and put her hand on his for the first time, a rare moment of true sweetness from the woman John saw so vividly reflected in the newly opened eye of his heart.

John passes into the cemetery behind the last car of the procession. He is aware now. Forest Lawn. Somewhere in the ground is his mother.

At 7:30 p.m., John and Zola got to their seats at the Yes concert that Zola had agreed to buy tickets for, so long as John paid for her bus ride as a condition for their first date. At two minutes and fifty seconds into "To Be Over," Zola turned and forcefully stuck her tongue down John's throat. It stunned him briefly but he responded in kind. The kiss was long and ugly.

"I want to get out of here," she said when it ended, her words reeking of alcohol.

"But the concert is not over yet."

"It ends when we say it does."

"Are you sure? I mean, these tickets couldn't have been cheap."

Zola's stance changed. "You're worried about money?" Her eyes were glazed. She stood back from him and angrily crossed her arms, teetering. "Okay then, John Harvey. Here I am telling you I want you, and here *you* are weighing the cost. So you decide. Right now. What is more valuable? I'll abide. We either go or we don't. It's up to you."

Six minutes later, John was losing his virginity in a portable bathroom in the parking lot of the stadium. Three weeks after that, John and Zola were engaged. Just a few mere feet from the red light now. Forty-seven miles an hour. Is that how she writes "happy"? It has been so long since he's seen it. He is trying to remember the last note Zola ever wrote him when Eleanor begins screaming. John looks up at her from the letter. She covers her face with her forearms. His eyes go back to where the road had once been but something has moved in front of it. John slams on the brakes and turns the steering wheel all the way to the left, in the opposite direction of the headlights that are barreling toward them. The oncoming Chrysler LeBaron slams on its brakes too and wrenches the wheel to the right, both of them now spinning away from each other through the dark in divergent rotations. Brakes howl. Headlights spiral like Catherine wheels. When the cars come to a stop, the drivers are yards apart facing each other.

"Oh my god," Eleanor says. "Are you okay?"

"I think so. Jesus Christ." John takes off his seatbelt and steps out of the car, intending to make sure the other driver is unharmed. But as he set foot to pavement, the Chrysler is thrown into drive and peels off down the street in the same direction it had been heading before it turned a complete 360 degrees untouched. As it passes, John makes eye contact with the driver and sees that one eye is brown and one is green.

He and Eleanor are quiet as they drive, she most likely recovering from the shock of the near impact and John still bewildered by the woman he is sure he saw at the wheel. The letter, for now, not the closest they had been to death. Cold air rushes in through an open passenger window and Eleanor looks up toward the moon. As they approach her place, a converted Italianate home on Fargo Street where she and David rent a two-bedroom apartment on the bottom floor, Eleanor finally speaks.

"Stop here. I'll walk the rest."

John turns off the headlights and pulls along the side of the street.

"You going to leave him?"

"No."

"I didn't think so."

"There's no one else for me, John."

John nods. "Okay."

"Thank you for picking me up. If I had to walk home, I'm not sure I would have made it back."

Eleanor kisses him on the cheek and gets out of the car. She closes the door lightly and walks toward her place with her arms folded at her chest, cradling a freshly wounded heart. In the passenger seat where she had been, the note. John folds it up, puts it back in the envelope, and stuffs it in his coat. Then he drives home, trying hard but unable to ignore the shrieking, flailing, sick truth inside his pocket.

The procession comes to a halt, and though the snow hasn't let up at all, the visibility is improving. John stands by a tree a few yards away from the row of cars, intending to see without being seen. A priest is already at the head of the grave. How long he has been there John is not sure. A man and a child emerge from the second car of the motorcade. The boy looks to be about ten. He has messy black hair. There is no emotion on his face whatsoever. Not sadness or anger or grief or despair. The man is in his thirties. He has not shaved nor combed. His expressions are languid. Neither of them wears coats or hats or gloves. Without taking his eyes from the burial plot, he shuts the door behind him and walks toward it. He does not wait for nor guide the child who walks alone a few feet behind him. No other car doors open. No other people arrive.

When John gets back to his place, he can see the walls flickering with color through the front bay windows. Zola is still on the couch in the living room by the door. He will have to enter through the back, but she sleeps deeply when drunk, so he isn't worried about rousing her and having to explain where he is coming from. John parks the car in front of the two-car garage behind the duplex and enters their bottom-floor apartment through the back into the kitchen. He closes it behind him and walks carefully across the room to a door that leads to the basement. He creeps down the stairs and across the cold concrete to the far wall. Between the bookshelf and a tool cabinet, a little below eye level, John removes a loose brick, reaches into the cavity, and pulls out a box. He opens the box, puts the letter in, puts the box back in the hole, and replaces the brick. Then he goes back upstairs and down the hallway to their bedroom. All of this is done in a trance. He won't remember doing it at all.

John climbs into bed. He tries to clear his head of the possibilities screaming out to him from behind the wall beneath the floor but sleep will not come. There is a word scrawled on the inside of his mind that separates him from waking life.

*Secret.*

He takes the word apart. He analyzes the pieces and reassembles them. He holds the whole thing up against the light. He puts it next to the ones he knows for certain. But this one, the one he saw in the letter that is now only in his mind, lost something on the trip from his periphery to his focus. It has degraded too much for him to be absolutely sure it was the same, his fear dragging it recklessly across the gravel to get it home before it faded out.

Of course, he could ask Zola if she had written it, but there is no outcome preferable to the momentary safety he has while in hiding. Were she to say "no," he may have his love in tact, but he would be forced to confess how he obtained the letter and possibly show his hand in regards to the feelings for Eleanor. He would also have to admit that he feels Zola capable of treachery, an admission that could rightfully drive her away. If she confesses, however, he would have his answer, but would never love again. And is that what he desires? To clutch the seed of certainty as he wanders barren land, every day a tedious journey away from woe across a scorched earth? No, John can't look. He will not dare risk unleashing the gruesome plague of proof that stands to spread extinction across his earth. The letter will stay folded up, hidden in darkness.

*It doesn't have to be. You just look away.*

When they reach the gravesite, the man takes his place at the left hand of the priest with his back to John. The boy stands across the coffin from him, his eyes cast downward. The two mourners give no indication they are related. No sign they share this loss. In fact, had they not arrived in the same vehicle, John would believe they didn't even know each other. Of course, they do not know John is there thinking anything at all. He is not their concern.

Down the hallway in the living room, Zola is also lying awake. She has been waiting for John to return, knowing there is something she must do immediately if the dates are to make sense. When she is sure the tears have stopped, she collects herself and goes toward the bedroom where John is lying senseless in an inconceivable quiet. She doesn't stand in the doorway exuding beauty, she doesn't speak to him of any desire, she doesn't flow naturally into his arms. Instead, Zola Lumi stumbles drunkenly over to the man lying on his back and mounts him. She does not remove any of her clothes. Burying her face in between his neck and shoulder, Zola reaches between her legs to get a firm grip on John's penis. John doesn't make a sound, his hands trembling with rage at his side as he stares out the window near the foot of their bed. When she thinks he is erect enough to comply, she slips aside her shorts and panties and stuffs him into her dry vagina. John grunts in discomfort and when Zola does the same he can't help but wonder if she did it mockingly. That tone of hers, the same dull fluctuations of toxic fumes that carried ridicule to him through the floors of his own home on the night she got drunk with her friends. He lies still as Zola moves her hips in circles. If there is any movement from him at all, it is only because those vibrations still ring him like a bell.

She had invited a few work friends over on a Friday, saying she needed a night with the girls and asked if he could either go out with his own friends or "work on something" in the basement.

"I don't have friends," he reminded her.

"What about Bill?"

"Bill?" John asked. "Who is Bill?"

"I don't know. You're always talking about a bunch of guys named Bill."

"*THE BILLS?*"

"Yeah, call those guys."

"I'll be in the basement."

When the women arrived, John led them into the kitchen, where Zola was drinking wine and preparing appetizers. He sarcastically offered his services but knew he was useless and went back downstairs to a small room in the basement to fiddle with the severed parts of a broken record player or read a book or whatever it was he did down there when nobody was supervising.

John sank into his barrel chair and picked up a book about exegetical fallacies that he had stolen off a clearance rack outside B. Dalton's. John had never stolen anything before, but on that afternoon he and Zola were in a hurry and a little buzzed from the lunch wine and she convinced him that the time it would have taken to go back inside and purchase it was worth more than the ten cents the store was asking for the book. In that moment, he threw caution to the wind, though the guilt had since pained him. John flipped to a dog-eared page and tried to pick up where he had once left off many months ago, but the words refused to fall in line. Not because it was a subject he had difficulty grasping or even that he had forgotten what he had read so far. Neither of those were true. The problem was that he could see only Enid. She was a thin woman with delicate pale skin, short, dirty blond hair, and light freckles like grains of sand smattered on pronounced cheekbones around a small elfin nose. They worked together and once in a while exchanged niceties in passing, but in his fantasies John knew her well. In the workplace, she was gentle and nervous. In his private thoughts, she was aggressive. Seductive. And tonight she was above him, in his kitchen. It clouded his mind with lust.

John tried to focus on his reading, tried to push Enid from his mental space, but she refused to be ignored, waving and smiling nervously at John from across the break room, leaning against the countertop by the coffee machine with her feet crossed, blowing on a hot cup of coffee. John glanced up from his book at a cracked brick in an adjacent basement wall. He shifted positions in his chair and read the same sentence for the fifth time, trying desperately to get the words in meaningful order, but he couldn't because he knew that behind the brick there was a box and in that box were photographs that the developers in Building 64 had deemed "too obscene" to return to their owners, photographs that were rescued from the furnace and traded around by the technicians in John's building—Building 61—like baseball cards. In one of those photographs there is a woman. She is on her hands and knees looking back into John's eyes through a pair of horn-rimmed glasses, biting her lower lip. Her skin is pale and her hair is short and blonde. The woman who is not Enid to anyone except John is on a red silk sheet. There is a man's finger inside of her.

John gave up trying to concentrate. He put the book down, stood up, and walked across the room. Removing a loose brick from the wall, he quietly withdrew a shoebox. Under the cover he found the picture facedown at the top of a heap of others. Not all of them were as graphic as the one he had come to know intimately, but they were all glimpses into people's most secret moments, and John was trespassing in one no less than in any other. He didn't belong there, in those bedrooms or those cars or those bathrooms with those couples. None of the women in the photos knew he was there, peering in. None of the men who took them could have guessed that their eyes would be possessed by an outsider, their perspectives hijacked in the cold and impersonal way that someone named John Harvey had hijacked them. Those moments were private. But John had pulled them out of the lives they once belonged to and held them captive behind a wall in his own home. One day, those nameless people might begin to forget that they ever happened. They'd faintly remember taking a few naughty photos the first time they went camping in The Catskills, but because the photos were never returned to them, the weight of the moment will blur and shift shape until it is just an unspecific impression left on a weakening human mind and they will lose their time like the melody of an old song. But John would not. He would revisit the remote island, one separated from context as a weak ox might become separated from the herd, and he would shamefully pleasure himself in a room hidden away from his wife while sneaking into a day that wasn't his.

He flipped the picture over. It was exactly as he remembered. The man's left arm is thick and hairy, and he is wearing a watch with a black leather band. The woman is still looking through him at John from inside the picture, out across who knows how many years or over how many miles. He took the picture into a closet in the basement where the laundry was and pulled a dirty sock from a pile of unwashed clothes.

The woman on the bed wiggled her ass at John, tempting him, daring him. The wristband on the watch of the man was now stainless steel. Oyster link. John removed his finger and took her tiny waist in his hands made enormous by comparison. She looked back and up at him, pleading with her eyes. John, a brand-new behemoth, towered over her powerless form. He dropped his pants down around his ankles and began to masturbate. Small, violent, and non-rhythmic jerking motions like that of a trapped fly, his hand not so much passing over his limp penis pleasurably as yanking any loose skin repeatedly in the vague direction of where his red testicles ought to be under an undulating tarp of off-yellow belly fat. He pumped furiously. As he did, his face grew hot and tight. John closed his eyes and conjured isolated samples of Enid's voice to make one coherent erotic statement.

"Hello, John. You. Are. Good. And. Big."

He felt his armpits getting moist. John pounded faster as his aloof unit swelled and stiffened in his tightly clenched fist. But just as the pink tip of his crooked hard-on peeked out from the tangle of pubic ivy that spread out over his hunched body from a cavernous naval, a new sound seeped into his fantasy. His own name, spoken from above. He tried to ignore it, closing his eyes tighter to bring Enid closer. No use. His name again. Not just spoken now. *Spit.* Muttered with a disdain that John could feel in his bones. The image faded and John's erection lost blood. It was Zola's voice. Though he couldn't make out her other words, the waves they traveled on were low and awful and turned the air they moved through into frozen water. Then there was laughter. Multiple tones. Enid's was among them. They were mocking him. He didn't know what about, but he was certain they were. When his penis had fully deflated, John shamefully pulled his pants back up and sulked back over to his chair.

On the verge of orgasm and not wearing a condom, John hurriedly tries to pull himself out of Zola, but Zola pushes back in protest against his withdrawal, and he ejaculates weakly inside of her. When his brief spasms have ceased, she sits up straight.

"Why did you do that?" he asks.

"Because I love you," she says, climbing off of him. Then she goes to the bathroom. John is asleep before she can return, but then she never actually returns.

The priest opens the Bible and begins reading. John cannot hear him. From where he stands by the bare maple, he can faintly see a large floral wreath staked into the ground with three thin, silver legs on the side nearest the boy. In the middle of the wreath is a photo of a woman. The dead woman, presumably. In the photograph she is on a beach. She is holding her left wrist behind her back with her face pointed up at the sun, eyes closed. She looks to be in her mid-forties, but her shoulder-length hair is silver. There are soft wrinkles near her eyes. Her pants are cuffed and her feet are in the water, but she is wearing a bright blue down vest over a blue-and-orange flannel shirt. It is the end of summer and the sky is made a lush, ardent pink by the warm sun that nestles into the horizon off camera. She reminds him of his own mother, also a resident of this sprawling dominion of soil, though John does not know in exactly which room she sleeps. He did not attend the funeral, nor has he spoken to any of his relatives since the accident. They no doubt consider John a villain. Like his father, they probably spoke his name with searing contempt, if at all, and thought him a petty coward who would not come to Astrid's bedside in her last days because he was aggrieved at a poor old woman for her honesty. The widower of a no-good bitch who abandoned his parents in their time of true grief to mourn the loss of an infatuation he mistook for love. But only John knew what she said to him in the hospital waiting room. No one else, even in their strangest and most forbidden perversions, could possibly imagine such cruelty.

Zola and his parents, particularly his mother, had a toxic relationship from the beginning, which only decayed with the passing of time until the very end of Zola's life, at which point it was an unsalvageable tangle of microaggressions. John's mother saw the woman—his first and only girlfriend—as an "insidious tramp" incapable of loving her son the way she felt he ought to be loved and a parasite that took advantage of his selfless naïveté. According to her, women like Zola were not to be domesticated, too dangerous and unrefined were her sensibilities, too vulnerable to impulse and extremes was her soul. She was seen instead as a lone wolf, a devil, disrespectful of their family's tradition, resentful of the bond between mother and son, and driven through the uncultivated terrain of her primal, immoral life not by common sense but by heightened senses—those of hunger, lust, and pleasure, dragging their weak, unworldly boy with her like a cub by the neck; a good boy, with unextraordinary dreams, deserving of a life of even keels, shielded from the elements and kept free of unnecessary pain.

To Zola, Astrid was a nosy authoritarian with an obsession for John that bordered on sexual; a stern woman with remarkable natural beauty for someone so petty and mean. She had been exceptionally overprotective of her large but fragile young son, and as a result of his exposure to the cruel children who mocked him for his enormity and awkward shyness, Astrid decided early on to shelter him from everything. Just to be safe. To her, it was better her boy know nothing than know suffering. As far as Zola was concerned, this was on par with the most heinous crimes, worse than even the mockery such a gentle boy had to endure. She could not comprehend a human being kept purposefully from experience, even the troublesome ones—especially a kid as clever and charming as John must have been. And so, as Astrid found purpose in keeping John in, Zola found hers in pulling him out. She had cast a spell on him, and Astrid would make it her mission to undo the bewitching. A tug-of-war indifferent to the strain put on the rope they pulled.

When John convinced Zola to move into his apartment, where she could live without the burden of rent or bills, his mother's disapproval became louder and more frequent, and the stress caused John to lose a considerable amount of weight. He also started drinking regularly as a way to cope with living an anxious life stuck between the only two women that had ever loved him. His mother, rather than admit she may have contributed, saw the dramatic changes to her son's appearance and behavior as evidence of "that slut's witchery."

But Astrid also failed to realize that by so openly disapproving of his new girlfriend, she and Major were only chasing their newly independent son further into the wilderness. John may not have been young, but young mutiny had been building in his prisoner's soul for many, many years.

So when suddenly there arrived an older woman, unpredictable but with a keen capacity for bliss, and as wise as she was passionate, John was so enamored by the newness that he could not help but to surrender. Zola was the embodiment of teen spirit, the key to the door, and though John was already in his early twenties, he found himself enlisting in the half-assed suburban revolution of all ordinary teenagers. Like most youth in revolt, John's nervous energy and freedom had begun to shape a new sense of self. Unlike most, he was an enormous man.

But in the private moments, the quiet ones, when John was not distracted by the chatter of combat between Zola and his family, he felt he was an imposter, a trespasser, lacking the intuition of a free spirit and unable to appreciate beauty. He doubted whether he was built for a battle of any magnitude and slowly grew to hate himself for the ways in which he had disappointed his mother, particularly when the voice in his head whispered of adultery whenever he thought about the letter, which was often. Until he met Zola, John was a sheltered, passive, and considerate man. But he had been awakened by an urge for self-actualization and lured out of the nest by a song he could not ignore. Now, out on the limb, he questioned if he could ever find a balance between obedience to his mortal family and fidelity to the immortal Zola. He wondered if maybe he had left too soon, equipped with the dream of flight but cursed with only one wing. Remorseful over the power of his own new heart, John never even told his parents he and Zola had married.

As the casket is lowered into the ground, the man begins to cry. He reaches into his jacket pocket and pulls out a flask. The chrome plating glimmers as he turns it upside down between his pursed lips. The child remains unflinching.

But when John was forced to break the news of Zola's pregnancy to his mother and father, Astrid and Major did not respond with anger, as John had expected. They didn't tell him they were disappointed or reprimand him or call her names or disown him or even shed a tear. What they did instead was far more cruel. Inconceivably so. They ignored her. Astrid would call the house often in the weeks that followed to check in on John and "their little boy," as she had begun referring to their unborn grandson. She made plans that did not include the child's mother. She bought large gifts in preparation without consideration for the wants or needs of the parents. She visited unannounced, but only when she knew Zola would not be home—and if she happened to return early, Astrid refused to grant her the kindness of eye contact. When Zola spoke, they dismissed her, looked through her, and when John tried to introduce some decency into the bizarre performance, Astrid feigned offense, suggesting that maybe he should stop drinking and get some rest. Brick by brick, Astrid rebuilt the division between her son and the world and she would not stop until he and Zola had lost sight of each other completely.

The priest scatters earth atop the coffin at the bottom of the grave. He bows his head to the man, then to the boy, then turns and walks until he is cut off from sight by the tree line.

The man stumbles back to the car that he and the child arrived in. Once he is inside and the door is closed, it and all other cars in the procession pull out of the grounds and are gone. The boy remains. John stays by the tree. He doesn't know how long they will both stand there or where either of them will go next, but for now the sight of someone else abandoned in the ether gives him comfort, gives his eyes something real to focus on. Minutes pass. John watches the boy, the boy watches the grave, no one moving. Then the boy looks up. He is aware of John's presence. Worried he might run the boy off, John reveals himself.

When Zola is six months pregnant, a malignant suspicion that has been festering inside of John takes shape and makes itself known. As he sits on a bench awaiting his bus on a warm afternoon in October, a gruesome thought strikes him. It is loud and articulate and unmistakable, and in its claws John is taken to a place worse than hell. Hell has answers. You know why you're there and that damnation is limited to eternity. But where John now languished, where this notion moved him, was a waiting room with no windows. No clocks. It gave no hints. Hell at least attended to its residents. But here, in his new doubt, John would sit untouched. Ignored. Watching.

"It is not yours," she said.

Without breaking eye contact, the boy reaches down and picks up some snow with his small, bare hand and tosses the loose flakes into the grave in the manner of the priest scattering earth. As he does this, the wind picks up, moving a patch of fog between them.

"Please," John says. "No more."

Having sensed annihilation, John becomes driven and severe. He is there for Zola but never really present. He is considerate but not kind. He takes her to all of her appointments, he paints the room, builds the crib, and buys the toys. He takes the pregnancy preparation class at the hospital and packs the overnight bag, and though Zola is not alone, she must have been lonely. But John is too task-oriented to notice. He is busy preparing the home for his child, his child, *his* child, his child, arranging, building, fortifying, protecting himself from the cataclysm that sniffs at the cracks in his brain.

The boy does not heed John Harvey. He has been readying himself for this moment for time immemorial and the fierce momentum driving him on will not be deterred by the whimpering of man. He reaches down, grabs another handful, and tosses it in as though stacking another brick, adding another corner to turn. The snow falls harder. To John, the boy begins to vanish. To the boy, John vanishes, too. The icy walls entombing him in his labyrinth of white wind multiply in number and size. He pleads again from deep within the ruins of its twisting, eternal confusion but his voice only reverberates off the stinging flurry and echoes mockingly around his head. The last thing John Harvey sees before his collection of peculiar impressions are erased from the record is the gray outline of a child scattering snow over a world at the bottom of a hole.

John is told his son is dead. He was right. It doesn't have to be.

"That whore killed our little boy," says Astrid.

One day. No shadows. All the time.

# CHAPTER EIGHT

COMING TO AGAINST THE TREE, BLOTTED OUT BY THE WHIPPING gusts of an almost concrete snowfall, John tries hard to remember exactly how many steps he took before turning with the motorcade into the cemetery so that he might be able to determine a way back out. Normally the recollection of otherwise useless detail was John's bent, but the blizzard had removed all context from the occurrences of the world and he knows that a step forward is the same as a step backward is the same as a step in place. Without measurable distance over which something happens, everything happens at the same time on top of everything else. Pure white omnipresence. Every hour combined.

*Just pick a direction and walk. Up or down. Back or forth. In or out. Doesn't fucking matter anymore. The roads don't connect anything anyway.*

The storm pushes him in the direction of the tree line, the same way the priest had walked when the service ended. It isn't toward the road, which John would have preferred, but where he goes next is not John's decision. He moves because the weather compels him to.

Minutes in the cold take centuries and the pain that pulses through his entire body keeps him conscious of every single agonizing one of them. Hours have passed. They must have. And yet there is no indication a single second's worth of change has happened at all. John is stranded. He is tired and estranged and he wants to go home. He doesn't care what ghosts linger there. He doesn't care that everything he sees inside of that cursed apartment drags him through the elaborate circuitry of his memory toward an underwater lake of old pain. At least his past is tangible. Bright. Familiar. This storm, though. This vacant stasis of pure white nullity that hints at no future is too bizarre for him to endure much longer. His eyes ache. His muscles scream from all the shivering and his empty stomach turns. John thinks about the sandwich waiting for him at Brinks, the one he asked Dinah to watch over, and he is spurred on by a ravenous hunger. If he hasn't gone back to retrieve either one, maybe they're both still there.

*Schrödinger's Sandwich.*

The muted green light of a Genesee Cream Ale sign. It strains to reach him through the briary tangle of snow, but when it does, it is as beautiful and warm as a crackling fire on a hearth. Brinks's neon, a beacon of the life-affirming despair that John has longed to return to since the moment he departed, should not be where it is, but it is nonetheless there, and John feels safe for the first time in his adult life. He speeds up his walk toward it, wheezing as he nears what might be considered a slow jog, and the sign gets brighter and larger and clearer until finally John has pulled it to a fixed position directly above him. He stands under it in awe, basking in the heatless green light of the most gorgeous beer sign he has ever seen. And he doesn't even like Genesee Cream Ale.

Remembering the snowball attack that took place in that very spot earlier in the day, John moves closer to the stairs lest another one come careening down the same path the earlier one had carved out, however many hours ago that was. He looks down at the bandage around his wrist and for one second laments the loss of his watch. For just one second, he wishes he had access to a constant in this ever-shifting city, and as he imagines how his day might have differed with minutes marking distance, he notices a glimmer on the ground of the endless, scrambled earth. Something peeking out of a drift. John reaches down to take hold of the curious protrusion, and when he brushes the snow off of it, he finds the chrome-plated knob handle of his walking cane. Thankful, John holds it tight and hobbles inside.

Brinks is empty. No patrons, no bartender. Not even a song on the jukebox. He calls out, his voice bouncing between the exposed stone peering through the ripped vinyl floor and the mineral fiber of the dropped ceiling, but no one responds. Solitude is not something he has ever associated with his beloved local haunt, and though he typically prefers to be left alone, John is in much need of some company. He takes his seat, third from the end, and waits. He knocks the bar with a closed fist and spins on his stool to scan the room. Finally there is a shuffling beyond the far wall and Dinah emerges from the basement carrying a case of beer, cursing at whoever interrupted her restocking. What she sees baffles her.

"Holy shit, John Harvey."

"There you are," he says, annoyed. "I thought I was going to have to serve myself." He twists back to face forward and catches a glimpse of a man in the mirror next to the register. He is strange, but not unknown. John has seen him before, but he certainly didn't expect to see him here now.

Dinah puts down the beer and folds her arms around his neck from behind.

"I'm so sorry, honey. So sorry," she says.

John takes her hand and unwraps her arms like dripping tendrils. "Jesus, Dinah, it ain't that big of a deal. I just want a drink."

Dinah steps back, an elbow on the pine, and puts her hand on his. In the humble illumination of the beer cooler that creeps out to them from across the bar, Dinah looks so much older than she ever has. Her wrinkles more pronounced, her hair streaked with thick gray. Her eyes sunken and tired.

"If you need anything at all from me. Anything," she says.

"Okay, let's start with the drink I just asked for twice already."

"You got it, baby. I'll get you your drink." She squeezes his hand lovingly and walks to the front of the bar and lifts up the hinged portion that allows her behind it.

"You're fucking with me and that goddamn door. I knew you repainted it."

"Painted it? You think we do upkeep in this shithole?" she says, walking toward him. "We have never repainted anything. We don't even plunge the toilets."

Dinah stops opposite him, behind the old, warped wood. Between them, the small letter X that John had once drunkenly carved with his house key to mark the spot at the bar where he always sat, the destination at the end of a long and winding walk.

"Whaddaya need?" Dinah asks.

"Hmm," John begins. "Today I think I'll try the exact same thing I have every fucking day."

Dinah forces a smile.

"Where are the boys? Don't tell me they all left already."

"Haven't seen 'em in a while. I'm sure they'll end up here eventually."

John looks around the empty bar. This place of great comfort now leaves him feeling unwelcome.

"Yeah, they always do." Dinah puts the drink down in front of John as he pulls the last cigarette out of his pack. "Fuck, I forgot to get smokes. *And* I got sober. Wasted all that money tryna get good and tanked and for what? Right back where I started." He lights it. "I know I promised myself I wasn't going to look today but I desperately need to know. What time is it even?"

Dinah shakes her head and grabs a tall glass from the shelf. "I'll tell you what I tell every paying customer who asks that question. It's whatever time you need it to be to stay right where you are buying drinks. Want me to turn up the game?" Without waiting for an answer, Dinah reaches up to the TV hanging above the register and twists the volume knob. Her blue sweater crawls up her back and the sight of her skin reminds John of his purpose.

Rick Jeannearette's voice booms out over the empty dive. The Sabres are losing to the North Stars, 4-1.

"Goddammit, Barrasso, get your fuckin' head outta yer ass," John yells.

A bell rings and the front door opens and Bertie limps in. Leo is following close behind. Bertie makes his way toward the middle of the room, but Leo's walk ends at the first seat as always.

"Fuck you guys go?" John yells. "Got called into work?" He laughs to himself and throws a few dollars on the bar next to the drink.

"Shit no, Mr. Harvey," Bertie stammers.

"We just, uh..." Dinah shrugs at him. "Stepped out to get some air."

He takes his place a few stools away from John.

"And a costume change?"

"Huh?" Bertie looks down at his purple and black pullover baja. "Oh. Gift from my grandkids."

"Yeah, well, I hope they got you two of them things. One to shit on and the other to cover up the shit with."

Dinah smiles nervously. Leo looks up and points a trembling finger at John. "When they let you out?" he asks. Dinah quickly pops the top off a beer and slams it down in front of him, positioning herself between Leo and John.

"You want me to keep these comin' today?" she interrupts.

John looks toward Leo and says, "Are you talking to me?"

"Yes, dear," Leo says back.

"No, he ain't talkin' to you," says Dinah. "Old man's confused. You know how it gets with these assholes. Drank a hole in their brain."

"More hole than brain at this point," John says as he takes a sip. The drink hits his tongue like battery acid. "Fuck, Dinah. You trying ta kill me? I wanted a whiskey and coke. Not rum."

"I'm sorry, honey. I'm all over the place. Been a long day. Ain't that right, Bertie?"

"Huh?"

"Jesus Christ, get a hearing aid already. I SAID, IT'S BEEN A LONG DAY, AIN'T THAT RIGHT?"

"Yeah. Oh yeah," says Bertie. "Longest I can remember."

"Hell of a storm out there," John says.

The door to the bar opens and a couple John has never seen before enters. New patrons are rare at Brinks because you don't just happen to walk by it. You need to have intent. You need to get in your car and drive the maze of one-way streets leading there and find a parking spot and pay the meter and go inside. You have a plan. You seek it out purposefully because you are hiding from disaster. The locals who had already staked their claim to it tended to be territorial, meaning that if someone new did happen find them there, they usually never found their way back. So when an old man and woman shamble through that door, John thinks it is one of the oddest things he had seen all day, and that is saying a lot. The man is wearing an ill-fitting black suit and tie and orthopedic shoes and the woman is in a long black dress with a pillbox hat on top of her white hair. She has white silk gloves on. They are both very somber, so John thinks they too must be coming from a funeral. The hunched old man has one arm around the waist of his wife and the other in her gloved hand and he escorts her to a dirty seat at the bar next to Bertie. When she arranges her weak, crooked bones on the stool, the man stands next to her with his hands folded behind his back. Dinah welcomes them pleasantly though they barely acknowledge her or John or Bertie next to them for that matter. They do not order drinks. They do not speak. Instead they stare directly ahead at the television. John is insulted that he is not acknowledged by the rookies as a veteran of Brinks. He has put hard time in. It doesn't matter that they are twice as old as he, there is a hierarchy in hell, and tourists are at the bottom.

When the door opens again and another couple enters, younger though this time, and also sit at the bar facing forward without saying a word to the men who had been on those front lines, who have dedicated their lives to this sin, John feels obligated to speak up. It is his duty to introduce himself as the ambassador of the wasteland and inquire as to their intentions before allowing them to pass.

"Da fuck is isss?" he blurts out instead. The old woman shushes him. Her husband with the withered face turns to him in disbelief. Dinah, who is leaning against the bar with her arms crossed looking up at the television, peers over at him in amazement and then narrows her eyes and tightens her lips. They all shake their heads. John is incredulous. He is about to say something more, louder this time and more specific, when the door opens again. Three middle-aged women saunter in. They too are dressed more formally than anyone ever was at Brinks. They too go right up to the bar and stare at the television. They too are silent.

They arrive infrequently at first, but the slow leak of solemn visitors eventually wears a hole in the door of the bar and soon people John Harvey has never seen in his life or ever cared to see are steadily streaming in. Some men are pale with combed hair and trimmed mustaches who mill about nervously. Some women smoke cigarettes and reapply their dark lipstick in handheld mirrors. He looks down the bar for Bertie or Ralph or Orson to get a read on their reaction to the unusual assembly but sees only Leo, piercing eyes glaring back at him in confusion while his old body is crowded toward its center by a bearded fat man in a tweed field sports jacket obsessively adjusting and cleaning his tiny, gold, round glasses, compressing Leo into a point in the distance like a raft diminished by a surging wave. Some of the newcomers greet each other cordially. Women kiss each other on the cheek. Men shake hands and pat shoulders. John watches each one closely and notices that after the initial greetings, no one ever speaks to each other again. They just huddle as close to the bar as they can get and stand there, all facing forward, all waiting quietly for the same thing to happen.

John grows restless as the room shrinks around him, one that, though filling like an hourglass, is forcing him further into isolation with every passing minute. Stranger still, he seems to be the only one bothered by the lack of room and the uncanny quiet that fills it. He considers breaking the silence with a song from the jukebox but decides that if he stands up, he will lose his coveted seat at the bar and he can expect no one to honor the marking he had made to claim his rightful position. Surrounded by an excitable audience awaiting something remarkable, John is left with no room to wander. In fact, there is barely enough room for him to turn in his place. Finally, his curiosity gets the best of him, and as much as he detests small talk, he decides he will try to glean an answer from a man next to him with the shaved head and a large red beard.

"Hey, buddy," John says, tapping his shoulder. The man turns and looks John directly in the eyes. He is frighteningly large and he does not look pleased about being bothered. "What's going on here tonight? You all here to watch the game or something?"

The man does not respond. He does not so much as blink. John notices a slight tremor in his lip. He begins to slowly grind his teeth.

"We are trying to concentrate," the man says. His voice is low and grim.

"On what exactly?" John asks.

"Our seven," he says, then gently closes his eyes, smiles serenely, and turns to face front. John doesn't want to know anymore. It wouldn't matter. He is sucking whiskey off an ice cube, mumbling invectives, when Dinah's harsh voice booms across the bar.

"Quiet everybody. They're returning." Everyone in the room stops whispering and stands at attention. They close their eyes and straighten their backs and lock their feet together with their arms at their side in a military formation. The silence that overtakes the bar is dense and full, like it is underwater. John strains his neck to see the television, but his view is blocked by a child on the shoulders of his father, which might as well have been a statue. The entire room is fossilized. John swivels his stool around in disbelief, expecting to see at least one anomaly, one movement to indicate life. But he finds none. Not a blink. Brinks is full of people bereft of life.

And then, without warning, it erupts. Pure pandemonium. The reanimated crowd around him bursts awake, waving their arms screaming with rapturous delight. A champagne bottle is popped. The angry, bald man turns to John, his face now a rictus of elation, and takes him in his arms.

"It worked this time," he says into John's ear. "We brought them home."

The jukebox comes on, and the first couple through the door, the man and woman who could barely walk, begin to dance with the freedom of children. Fluidly and without compunction. A circle forms around them. Everyone hollers with delight as the man tosses his wife into the air.

*This is a place of mourning. Show some goddam respect.*

A woman places her hand on his right shoulder.

"Come dance with me, John Harvey," she says, her voice coming from somewhere in the frenzied horde. As confused as he is at the spontaneous vigor, he is relieved to hear his own name spoken aloud. It means someone knows him, can anchor him, commiserate with him. John frees himself from the constricting embrace of the over-delighted bald man but sees nothing recognizable in the undulating swamp of blissful alien forms.

"John," says the voice again. "It's me."

In front of him is a woman of remarkable beauty. Light skin, short blonde hair, at least a foot shorter than him, with small gray eyes behind black horn-rimmed glasses, wearing a white button-up shirt under a leopard-print jacket. But the way she asks him to join her, the shakiness in her voice, the concern in her eye, gives John the impression that she is being put up to this. A prank. And somewhere in the crowd, a group of women watch and snicker as their gorgeous friend teases the large, lonely man at the bar. He wonders how she could have known his name. Maybe a classmate. John takes the attendance of everyone in his middle school homeroom. Beads of sweat form on his upper lip. He cannot place her face. Maybe she is older. Meaner. Maybe she has a brother. Stronger. More cruel. Is he watching too? John scans the bar for any threatening individual who may be looking on waiting for John to make contact with his sister or his girlfriend or his wife, whoever she was that had been put up to this, giving a bully with an old grudge a new excuse to attack. He would be careful to give him none.

Venomously, John replies, "I don't dance, lady."

"Lady?" Her thin eyebrows furrow and she crosses her arms. "We used to dance all the time."

She *is* someone from his past. They had found him here. They had come back to torment him.

"You got the wrong guy. Please, just leave me the fuck alone."

The woman half smiles, hurt but probably more confused. John makes no movement. Thinking it maybe just a cruel joke, she wraps both of her tiny hands around one of his. John casts off her unsolicited touch.

"John, it's me. What are you talking about?" she asks mournfully, hoping that her plea, if made slow and deliberate, might rouse his memory.

"I'm not that kid anymore," John says. "Leave me alone. I don't want any trouble."

She is completely taken aback at his reaction. Looking around the room, mouth open, tongue tucked against her back teeth, the small woman's eyes begin to shine.

"Jesus, John. Am I that forgettable?"

But John is barely listening and his eyes dart back and forth across the room looking for those who may have been stalking him.

"The back staircase?" says the woman.

John shakes his head. "No," he says firmly. He doesn't know what she could have been referring to. He cannot remember what happened in a school staircase, but it was obviously so traumatic that he has blocked it out. John wipes the sweat off his forehead with the back of his hand and cracks his knuckles.

"The break room? Your car?"

John shrugs blankly and looks for a way out. He knows now for sure she is fucking with him, trying to suggest something arbitrary that might give John a false memory and allow the game to continue. But Dinah is approaching. His escape car.

"Nothing, John? You used to write me the sweetest notes. What happened to you? Where did you go?"

"I killed myself and came to hell. Like what I've done with it?" John gestures around the bar. A tear falls down the woman's face and she angrily smears it across her cheek.

"You're fucking horrible," she says, and returns to the swell.

John, unmoved by her madness, turns around. Dinah is there to meet him.

"How are you doing, honey?" she asks. "You holding up?"

John looks back over his shoulder at the woman in the corner. She is crying and alone. "I could use another drink."

"Please don't tell me you're drinking martinis now," Dinah begs. "I've made a hundred martinis already tonight."

"Martinis?" John is disgusted. "Who the fuck drinks those?"

"Happy people." Dinah puts a pint glass full of whiskey on the bar. She adds a splash of coke.

"Yeah, well…" He flips his lighter open and closed. Open and closed. Open and closed. "This world is not for them." Open and closed.

But John knows it is he who does not belong.

# CHAPTER NINE

B Y THE TIME JOHN HAS FINISHED THE DRINK, BRINKS IS BURSTING with unrecognizable life. Dinah is visibly flustered by the drink orders being shouted from all directions in all languages and John's mood has grown worse. He can't understand where all these fucking people have come from or why they have descended upon his position in the boundless white dream. There are so many other places they could have gone to spread out, but instead they have decided to spend the end of his longest day cramped into this tiny bar by his shitty apartment. He can no longer clearly hear the jukebox, which is now emitting only muffled clangs and fractured bits of an unrecognizable melody. Bertie and Ralph and Orson are gone from sight, Leo had forfeited his seat to a smoking woman with jet-black hair and bangs wearing a pink jacket of feathers, and Dinah has barely said a word to him in what must have been an hour.

He remembers that morning, his firm resolution to submit to every diabolical perversion of hers and how different she now seemed from the lustful bartender he had put up with for so long. It wasn't just an idea he had; it was a process he saw played out on a stage. The bar would be empty save for the locals who gathered around the television in the front to watch soap operas and drink tequila in the commercial breaks. Dinah would be tired and overworked, leaning against the register reading a magazine, the red light above her reflecting off the glossy pages and illuminating her devilishly from beneath. She would look up at him and smile and cock her head toward the beer cooler, wordlessly implying a quick fuck while all eyes were turned away, expecting him to say no yet again. But today he would say yes. Today he would abandon his grievous reputation, weave his vulgar shadows through her clammy hands and reappear as a man transformed by pleasure. He would have if all these people hadn't shown up to distract her. At no point in his plan had he been refused.

"John, are you crazy?" Zola laughed.

The coworkers at the party who happened to bear witness nervously shuffled and sipped their drinks. Some tried to look away but others stared directly at him. John got back to his feet.

"But."

Zola laughed again. The soft, fluctuating tonal pulses tapped against his glass heart like a tack hammer. "Oh honey. You're cute, but it is *way* too soon for that." She took his face in her hands and kissed his cheek and then went back to her conversation with Steve. She was still laughing to herself as he walked away.

He does not remember leaving the building. He does not remember the drive. He does not remember who he spoke to on the phone or what was said before he let the phone fall. He does not remember the walk through the kitchen to the bathroom. But he remembers the warmth.

*It ends when we say it does.*

"John?" Dinah says. "Can you please keep an eye on the place for me? I have to go grab some stock." She touches John's hand and brings him back and the room around him reveals itself like an image developed on film.

"Oh. Yeah, sure," he says as he pulls himself to the forefront of it. He looks at her hand on his. Her perspective. *That's* why John felt so compelled to surrender to her that morning. Dinah was eliminated from the discourse of the furies, had remained untouched by the passing of time that had so ravaged John. She knew what he knew and stayed aloft, high above the sorrow that weighed down his version of the earth, and possessed a fearlessness that staved off decay. John needed to occupy that space, her space—one not yet constricted by the cold. Dinah may be a vulgar woman, shameless and indiscreet, but there is something about her that not even her barefaced perversity can deter John from. It is what she sees and what she does not that stirs desire in the furthest reaches of his blood.

Dinah walks out from behind the bar, pushes her way through the crowd, and disappears behind the door to the beer cooler. Under the spell of drink, John stands, grabs his cane, and sets off after her, moving stealthily among the crowd, tracking Dinah's every step through the brambles of flesh and exuberant celebration to the door at the back corner. He takes one last glimpse around, knowing it will all be different when he returns.

He steps inside and makes his way down the stairs.

The basement of Brinks is mainly used for storage but doubles as a small office. Old kegs are stacked on the far-left wall and across the room on the right are shelves of liquor and industrial-sized cans and glass jars of food. In the middle of the floor is a card table where some of the guys would gamble and drink after the bar is legally supposed to lock its doors for the night, but it also serves as a desk for tracking the bar's finances. There is a calculator and rolls of receipt paper on it as well as a full ashtray. A calendar hangs on the wall next to the door. John sees that it hasn't been flipped since May of 1983. As filthy as it is, the fluorescent bulbs above the table make it feel, to John, oddly sterile. Through the room to the back is a walk-in beer cooler separated from the office by long, thick strips of heavy, translucent plastic. John can see the distorted image of Dinah moving some beer cases around behind them and he hears her swearing to herself.

He taps on a glass jar with the end of his cane.

"Hey, motherfucker!" she yells. "Employees only!" Bottles rattle in their case as she drops them to the floor.

Dinah comes out through the plastic in a rage, but when she sees John standing there, her demeanor changes entirely. "John, what are you doing here? I thought you said you would watch the place for me."

"I was," he says. "But it's running like a well-oiled machine. Thought I'd give you a hand."

He takes off his sunglasses and puts them into his shirt pocket and makes his way into the cooler. The cold clouds are blinding. Dinah looks at him curiously as he passes her and stands against the back wall. With her at the entrance, she appears to John drenched in shadow.

"John what are you doing?" Dinah steps toward him into the light. He thinks she looks very young and beautiful. He takes her hand and brings her closer.

"Oh, John. Honey," she says. Her voice full of pity. "This is a bad idea. It's way too soon."

"Why would it be too soon?" He looks at the place on his wrist where his watch had once been. "If anything, it's almost too late."

"There just...it hasn't been that long since..." Dinah speaks cautiously. "You know, I'm sure it still hurts."

"Jesus, Dinah," he says, letting her hand fall. "It's been years. A man's allowed to move, ain't he?"

Dinah looks puzzled. "Years? John, maybe you've had too much to drink. Let's get back up there. The inmates could have taken over the asylum by now."

"Just one more minute," John says, and kisses her without thinking another thought of any kind, which surprises them both. Dinah doesn't move at first but eventually she changes her mind and allows herself to meet him there. She grabs the back of his bald head under his hat and pushes her tongue farther into his mouth. He expects her breath to taste like beer or smoke, but it is neither. It is nothing. Her tongue is a cold, wet muscle of throbbing ice. John idiotically fumbles with her belt buckle. She pushes his hands aside and does it herself. Then she unbuckles his.

"Are you sure about this, John?"

"For now," he says.

"Good enough." Dinah turns her back to him and pulls her jeans down to her ankles. Then she places her hands flat against the wall and arches her back, pressing her big, soft ass into John's fully erect penis. He takes it in his hand and tries to insert it into her but feels only a flat, stone-like surface against his skin.

John looks down but he can't see anything below his waist. He is terrified. The frigid mist of the beer cooler is mud thick.

"Hurry up, John," Dinah says impatiently, her voice gruff and loud.

Panic-stricken at what he cannot find, he squints and tries to decipher the strange shape of her body, but the closer he looks the farther away she gets, separated from him by the swirling clouds of palpable gray froth that rise up between.

"What the hell are you doing back there?" she growls. "Put it in. Quick."

But John can't find his way into her. He considers running but a new airlessness grips his throat. He struggles to breathe as crystals of ice fill the grave they both stand in.

"John!"

His mind is broken. He cannot separate the layers of time that lie stacked like plates.

A unified and immoveable monolith of seconds takes all forms of matter at once, dripping and crashing and rising into each other without lapse, exchanging positions and depths according to the entropic chime of a divine, internal metronome. A blue coat falls onto the floor. Nature covers bones in muscle and fur and a new body is born from between the rocks. Flames return to the pieces of wood that arrange themselves into the walls of a remote cabin. Winter after winter after winter with no light or warmth in between. Fumes are pulled out of the air by a metal pipe and cooled into a liquid that sits still in a tank. A full moon ticks back and forth at the top of the sky. A growth uncoils itself from around a small neck in darkness and a heart begins to beat.

Looking for some point of reference, John uses both hands to trace Dinah's back, which feels ten feet long. When it eventually curves into her upper legs, there is nothing but smooth marble, bald and hard. A car reverses through a red light. Noxious sounds return to a stillness before the savage vibration starts. A fist withdraws from a hole in the wall. The hole closes.

"John, is that you?" A woman's voice from a dangling phone. The fog now a pulpy mass of off-white distortion that cushions John like a fragile possession in transit.

"Are you there?"

John turns away from Dinah in shock and tries to flee, but he can barely trudge through the maelstrom of slush that swirls around him. Her voice grows smaller and smaller behind the immense ringing in his ears, the long wail of a machine in mourning, the dreary hum of hard drugs. With all of his strength, he struggles to push his enormous body through the grinding waves, a quicksand of crushed ice that overwhelms the insignificant will of the insect at the helm, but he can barely move it. And just as he is about to be buried completely, he is pushed through to the surface and thrown against the hard forest floor. His nose cracks against it, his loose tooth finally coming out of his head. John picks it up and closes his hand tightly around it. The blood that pours from his broken nose is clear and thick and when it drips onto the snowy ground, it forms a puddle in which small islands of ice creak like closing doors as they collide. There is someone down there in the waves. She has returned. He tries to get to his feet but there is no room to stand. Then a pair of white boots appears.

John struggles like an infant to lift his head and look up. Above him, peering down from the gallows of an impartial winter, the Woman in White, each of her innumerable glass eyes a different shade in which John can see himself reflected as the arrogant child he is. He reaches for help, but she does not provide. Instead, she unzips her white coat and reveals a darkness so pure and final and vivid that even death looks uninspired. And there, in that blind spot of god, in the infinitesimally small room where the watchmaker keeps his shadows, a familiar voice.

John crawls inside and can be seen no more.